Private Lessons

Dara Girard

Private Lessons

Copyright © 2017 by Sade Odubiyi

ISBN 13: 978-1949764086

Printed in the United States of America
Cover photo © 2017 akz/123rf
Cover and Layout Copyright © 2017 Ilori Press Books, LLC

This is a work of fiction. Names, characters, places, and incidents either are the product of the author's imagination or are used fictitiously, and any resemblance to actual persons, living or dead, business establishments, events or locales is entirely coincidental.

ILORI PRESS BOOKS, LLC
PO Box #10332
Silver Spring, MD 20914

www.iloripressbooks.com

Other Books by Dara

The Black Stockings Society
Power Play
A Gentleman's Offer
Body Chemistry
Round the Clock

Return of the Black Stockings Society
Playing for Keeps
After Hours
A Private Affair
Just One Look

Henson Series
Table for Two
Gaining Interest
Careless Rapture
Dangerous Curves
Familiar Stranger

The Clifton Sisters
The Sapphire Pendant
The Amber Stone

It Happened One Wedding
Unexpected Pleasure
Midnight Promise
Sweet Temptation

Novels
Illusive Flame
Honest Betrayal
The Daughters of Winston Barnett
Remember My Name

Chapter One

Having coffee with her was not part of the plan. He didn't even like coffee shops—the noise, the smell, the people—or the coffee for that matter. He didn't even know why he'd said yes. He should have politely declined, but he hadn't and now he had to pay.

Dylan Flynn shifted his gaze from his white and brown cardboard cup filled with a nearly black liquid he didn't plan to touch, to his companion's drink, which looked more like a dessert than a beverage with the whipped cream piled high and dotted with chocolate sprinkles. He glanced at the glazed Danish that she'd ordered for both of them.

He didn't do sweets either. He lived a regimented life—boiled egg, toast and orange juice every morning—and rarely varied from it. But he wasn't acting like himself and hadn't been for the past month. It was Dylan Rodgers who'd said yes to a pretty woman, who drank coffee and the same man who was now out of a job.

It hadn't come as too much of a surprise after the arrest, but he didn't want to think about that right now (his brother-in-law, Malcolm had fallen over laughing when he'd had to bail him out), nor did he want to think about how close he'd gotten into further trouble.

If he had been thinking clearly he wouldn't have said the words that had gotten him here, "They say bad news comes in threes. I had to put my dog down yesterday and now I've lost my job, I wonder what's next." He hadn't expected her pretty brown eyes to widen in sympathy and then offer to take him for coffee where she had given him advice on other companies he could try. And that's when he realized getting fired was a lucky mistake because in a short period of time he'd started looking forward to his job and seeing her and that would have complicated things since his job was to spy on her and everyone at By Your Side. The idea had been his grandmother's.

He'd drawn the short straw for his grandmother's plan. He usually did. He did what others didn't want to do. His younger brother, Josh, was too emotional; his brother-in-law, Malcolm, too recognizable and his sister, Gwen…well nobody considered her for anything. "You've been in the background so nobody knows you," his grandmother had said as they all sat in the boardroom of the Flynn Fleet headquarters where she ruled. She sat at the head of the light pine table as if holding the attention of a small army.

"Mom, do you really think this is necessary?" his mother, Adelaide, said in a soft voice.

His mother always spoke softly in Elena Flynn's presence, as if in constant gratitude that she'd been allowed into the family. Elena had taken her time giving her consent that Adelaide be allowed to marry her beloved only son, Mauro.

Dylan had gotten his height from his mother, but she stooped her shoulders to appear smaller, her black hair had streaks of grey that would have made a more attractive, self-assured woman look distinguished, but instead just made her look old. She looked like the widow she was.

His grandmother, in contrast, had a shock of white hair, styled in a trim pageboy cut that only made her light brown features appear even more striking and youthful, like the scent of orange blossoms she liked to wear. She stood several inches shorter than her daughter-in-law, but commanded attention as if she dwarfed her.

Elena ignored her. "We have to find out what they're doing. No detail is too small."

"What if he gets caught?" Adelaide said, lifting her voice to just above a whisper.

Malcolm cleared his throat. Dylan noticed he always did that when he wanted to make a point. It wasn't a nervous habit but deliberately done to appear as if he were working up the courage, when, in truth, he was never without it. He'd worked at Flynn for more than ten years and had been married to Dylan's sister for nearly nine. Their union had produced a boy and a girl. He had the kind of corporate polish his grandmother loved. Good looking without being distracting, deferential without being oily and succeeded in making connections that were useful. "I have some data that—"

"I don't care about data," Elena said. "I don't like what I see. I don't like seeing them expand into areas that should belong to us."

He cleared his throat again. "I just—"

"This is not up for discussion. It's time that one of us find out the inner workings of that company. You keep doing what you do." She shifted her hard gaze to Dylan. "I'm trusting you. The success of our business depends on what you can find."

"But aren't we already successful?" Josh said. Unlike Dylan, his younger brother hadn't inherited their mother's height, but instead their father's more medium, stocky build. He had a round face and soft tones like his mother that generally irked his grandmother.

She bristled. Whether at his question or his soft tones Dylan couldn't tell. "In order to stay successful one must never become complacent. Haven't I told you that?"

"Yes, but—"

"We cannot allow them to get a stronger foothold in this community. And that ride along—"

"Sharing," Malcolm corrected.

She waved her hand in dismissal. "Why didn't we think of that?"

"We still have a strong market with our transport vans," Malcolm said. "We have to be careful about using a different model without—"

"You're giving me excuses not answers." She looked at Dylan. "And as usual you're staying mute about this."

He shrugged.

"You have nothing to say?"

He blinked.

She stared at him for a long moment, her dark green gaze, an indicator of her mestizo heritage in Nicaragua, challenging him to say something, but soon gave up and looked at the others.

"I don't see why you want to use Dylan when he's not really part of the company," Gwen said, twirling a long strand of dark hair around one of her manicured fingers.

Dylan shot his sister a look, wondering why she had to bring that up. His grandmother wanted him to work at the company like everyone else did; instead, he only occasionally consulted with them. He ran a separate company that invested in other businesses. He loved his sister but didn't particularly like her. She had a cruel streak and more than once he wondered why Malcolm had married her.

"He knows that soon he'll have to stop behaving like a child and take his rightful place." Elena met his gaze. "The place his father would like to see him hold."

Dylan rubbed his chin, trying not to yawn.

She frowned.

"Well, if that's everything," Malcolm said, glancing at his cell phone. "I have another meeting."

"That's all," Elena said.

Dylan nodded and went to the door. He was halfway down the dark carpeted hallway when he felt a grip on his arm that made him jump. He spun around and glared at his mother. "I hate when you do that."

"I said your name," she said in a tone of apology, taking a step back.

He took a deep breath; he didn't like getting angry at her. His father had made her fearful enough. "It's okay," he said in a softer tone, "but I've told you to speak up when you say my name."

"I'm sorry."

He turned and continued walking. "I'm in a hurry, what do you want?"

His mother hurried after him like a scared mouse. "You don't have to do this. You can say no."

He sent her a cynical grin. "Are you being serious?"

She rubbed her hands together. "At least you can try. I guess, I don't know. I don't want—"

He gently touched her shoulder. "I'll be okay."

"You don't have to keep taking the jobs no one else will."

"Why not?" Gwen said meeting them at the elevator. "He's good at it."

Dylan rubbed his eyes, wishing he'd brought his eye drops since his contacts made his eyes dry. "As opposed to being useless?"

She clicked her tongue unfazed. "Jealous because I married well?"

"I still wonder what Malcolm got in the bargain."

She curled her lip.

"Where is Malcolm by the way?"

"He decided to take the stairs."

"Yes, being with you in closed spaces would cause a man to run."

Adelaide shook her head. "You shouldn't say things like that Dylan, you'll hurt her feelings."

"Feelings?" Dylan said with a laugh. "You mean she has them?"

The elevator doors opened and they all got in.

"Everyone has feelings," Adelaide said gently scolding him. "You shouldn't tease her like that."

"I don't care, Mom," Gwen said. "I did my part and Gran likes me."

"Wait!" Josh called out running towards the elevator.

Gwen pushed the 'Close' button.

Dylan put his hand between the doors, stopping them and then shot her a look.

She shrugged. "He should use the stairs. He could use the exercise."

Josh stumbled into the elevator breathing heavy. "Thanks. I got caught with Gran."

"Poor boy," Gwen said, patting his back in a patronizing way.

Josh smiled at her not sensing her sarcasm. "Her idea is crazy, but there's no way to change her mind."

Adelaide cast a nervous look at Dylan. "Unless someone decides not to do it."

Dylan stared at the elevator numbers as the car slowly descended.

"She could be setting you up to fail. If anyone finds out—"

"I can take care of myself." *Always have always will.*

"Are you sure you want to do this?" Josh said.

"What's wrong with you two?" Gwen said. "You keep acting as if he has a choice. We all know Dylan's the guard dog."

"Gwen!" Adelaide said.

"I mean it as a compliment. He knows that."

The elevator stopped on the lower level. Dylan exited first hoping he could get to his car without further discussion. His brother had other ideas.

"I think Mom's right," Josh said, struggling to keep Dylan's pace as he headed to the front doors. "Gran isn't to be trusted."

Dylan waved goodbye to the security guard then opened the door to the autumn air. "You worry too much."

"I'm just not sure this is necessary. I looked over Malcolm's data—"

"No, what she has planned is not necessary, but it's something I have to do."

"Because Gran says so?"

He shrugged. "There's nothing wrong with seeing what our rival business is doing."

"But undercover?"

"It's a good way to see how things operate when they don't think someone is watching."

"I'm not saying it's a bad idea. I'm just not sure of the legalities…"

"I won't get caught."

"Plus..." He sighed and stopped.

"What? Go on and say it."

"I'm not sure you're the one to do it. You don't exactly blend in well. You're more of a 'behind-the-scenes' kind of guy."

His brother was right. Dylan wasn't known as a people person and preferred to be by himself, but he could observe and spot systems and patterns in businesses and his grandmother knew that skill was useful. And he liked to keep their grandmother happy enough to keep her out of his life.

"Do you want to take my place?"

His brother visibly shivered. "No."

Dylan stopped in front of his car, the scent of freshly turned soil from the Maryland farmlands surrounding the industrial park where the headquarters sat, drifting in the air. He looked and saw a cow grazing in a distant field under low hanging white clouds. As a child he used to watch cows feeling a kinship. He knew they weren't as stupid as they looked. He opened his car door and affectionately patted his brother on the cheek. "Relax and stop worrying, I've got this."

He pulled out of the parking lot onto the main road feeling as if he could start breathing again. He never felt himself when he had to be in the squat tan building that housed his grandfather's business. Jamaican born Berton Flynn had left his adopted home of Nicaragua with a new bride and son and headed to America for a new life. After twenty years of working for the same medical billing company he branched out on his own and started "Flynn's Fleet" a medical transport business more than thirty years ago and it had done very well. His father had briefly served as president until illness cut his life short and Elena took over.

Then ten years ago, By Your Side entered the market. They didn't think much of this new entity until they started losing some business. While working undercover Dylan saw firsthand how By Your Side's different business structure mirrored other more popular ride share programs.

While Flynn's Fleets provided medical transport primarily to individuals and facilities serving clients with disabilities, limited access and various medical needs, By Your Side had a different audience. The owner of the newer company had seen a growing group of active seniors who would pay for a different form of transportation. Seniors who could no longer drive, or didn't want to, signed over their personal vehicles in exchange for an 'on call' service that provided transportation for various errands such as grocery shopping, doctor appointments, clothes/gift shopping, visiting family and friends even trips to events such as the opera, plays, and sports games. Anywhere a person wanted to go.

By Your Side also had a fleet of vans that worked exclusively with select nursing and rehabilitation facilities, providing medical transport.

Their small community of Old Dayton could accommodate this bold plan and By Your Side was thriving, which made his grandmother nervous and with reason. If they wanted to stay ahead they needed to have the right information. Flynn's Fleets current model was far too limited and set in its old model and two straight quarters of declining revenue showed this.

Dylan sat back in his chair as a child squealed behind him and a coffee machine hummed. He'd enjoyed his undercover work and the people he'd gotten to know. Especially Jodi Durant. She had been a surprise. At first, he'd been taken aback by her age (early thirties), nail polish (blue), jewelry (studded piercing at the top of her ear, plus four others—two in each ear) and short, natural black hair, they weren't in line with the image he had of By Your Side. He'd imagined the clientele would feel more comfortable with a more conservatively dressed woman, settled comfortably in her middle years or older, but Jodi had quickly changed his assumption with one action: a smile.

The first time he'd been introduced to her, her mouth had spread into a smile as warm as a hug. People hardly ever smiled at him. If they did, they were usually timid, nervous or unsure, but this woman flashed a bright smile as if she planned to make him her new best friend.

"Hi, I'm Jodi and you'll be shadowing me today. I usually work in the office, but we had an unexpected emergency because two drivers got sick so I'm taking one of the driver's routes while we get a temporary driver to cover the other route."

To his annoyance he was actually tongue tied for a minute. He shook her outstretched hand while no words came out. "No need to be nervous," she said, her smile making his cheeks burn. "You'll be fine."

He was immediately under her spell. She made a person feel important; if his grandmother could clone her she could make a fortune.

During the one day he'd spent with her, he knew she was the key to the company's success. She shared with him how some drivers could be trained to also sit with clients at appointments and help with grocery shopping for those who didn't want deliveries. She was a fountain of ideas of how the business could improve and he'd filed away all of her ideas. He got to know the other drivers and the main office staff, but came to see that Jodi was the driving force. To his surprise he'd learned she'd come up with a unique design for clamping in wheelchairs and walkers, which the company patented.

But he wouldn't get to see her again. By next week he'd be back behind a desk. He took a sip of his coffee—black, no sugar, the way his father used to like it. He grimaced as the now cold bitter liquid hit his tongue then spit it back in his cup.

"That's disgusting," Jodi said with a laugh.

He wiped his mouth. "Sorry about that."

"You left it too long and now it's cold." She turned to the counter. "Do you want—?"

"No, I'm fine."

She turned back to him with a rueful smile. "I knew I should have ordered for you. I memorized everything on the menu."

"It wouldn't have helped."

"Why not?"

"I don't like coffee."

She laughed. "That's a good one."

"I'm serious."

She stared at him. "Really?"

He nodded, ready to be honest about something.

She slapped him on the arm. "Then why didn't you tell me? We could have gone somewhere else." She looked at his untouched Danish in dismay. "Do you hate that too?"

"No, just not hungry."

"This was supposed to be my treat."

"This is fine."

"But it doesn't make any sense. Why did you say yes to having coffee with me?"

He shrugged. "I'm still having a good time."

"But you don't like coffee."

"No, but I like you."

Chapter Two

Jodi knew it was dangerous to laugh. Dylan wasn't the kind of man you laughed at, but what had just come out of his mouth had sounded ridiculous. He liked her? This man who didn't look like he liked anything?

The first thing she'd noticed about him was his body. Not his height, he was tall, but no taller than most men, but she noticed his physique. He had the body of a laborer—broad shoulders, thick legs—the kind of man who looked like he could move timber by himself. He had features like a carved walnut sculpture and serious dark eyes that looked as cold as a frozen lake at night. He had a solitary driven presence which made his appearance at By Your Side strange. He didn't look like someone who liked to work with people, but after a few awkward moments he'd fit in.

She looked down at his Danish then back up at his face to see a change in his expression, but she couldn't read anything. Perhaps he'd been teasing her. Or maybe she'd misheard him. She opened her mouth to ask him to repeat himself, but the ring of her cell phone cut her off.

He stood. "You'd better get that."

"No, wait," she said, grabbing his hand. When he looked down in surprise, she quickly snatched her hand away. "What did you just say?"

"I said you'd better get that."

She shook her head. "No, before you said that. What you said about the coffee." Her phone continued to ring.

"I said I don't like coffee."

"No, after you said that—" She held up her hand. "Just wait a minute." She checked the number. "It's an emergency, but don't go anywhere, okay?" She didn't give him a chance to reply as she went outside so she could hear better. The popular coffee shop was too noisy.

When she returned moments later, she wasn't surprised to see him gone. The emergency had been easily remedied—a driver had gotten double booked—and had wasted her time.

She returned to her seat and sank down into the chair defeated. One of the most interesting men she'd ever come across had just walked out of her life. And he liked her.

Or had she just imagined it?

Who says something like that then just walks away? She sighed in disappointment. Yes, she must have misheard him. Perhaps she'd heard what she'd wanted to hear, that he'd felt the attraction too. She noticed he'd taken the Danish. She wondered if he'd eat it or throw it away.

Her attraction to him had come out of nowhere. Certainly not the first time she met him.

He wasn't her type, she hadn't even realized she had one until she looked at him and realized he wasn't anything like the kind of man she'd imagine falling for. He was far from conventionally handsome, and quiet, she preferred people who liked to talk, but she sensed something deeper there.

And she hadn't paid much attention to him until one day when he came into the office and saw her struggling with the replacement jug for the water cooler. He calmly took it from her and settled it in place. She thanked him and he looked directly at her, making everything around her fall away, and said in a low voice, "You're welcome, Jodi," and at that moment she was adrift in the frozen lake and strangely didn't feel cold. Instead her skin felt hot, her breath shallow.

No man had ever looked at her like that. Most men looked past her or through her, but his gaze hit her right at her core awakening something inside her that she hadn't known had been asleep.

"You're not serious," her friend and colleague Cara Manusco, said in surprise when Jodi shared how she felt one day after work. They enjoyed getting together at the local diner, a crowded place known for large portions and friendly staff. Cara wanted to stay away from her mother-in-law, who had recently moved in with her family and was staying for a few months. She'd recently cut her long brown hair short to annoy her husband. Jodi had agreed to meet her just so she didn't have to face another dinner alone. "You're going to ask him out?"

"Not on a real date," Jodi said quickly, munching on her tuna melt. "Just for coffee."

"Why?"

"Why not?"

Cara paused. "Besides the fact that he's scary?"

Jodi waved a French fry at her. "He's not scary."

"Don't play with your food."

Jodi ate the fry.

"And I stand by what I said. Come Halloween he doesn't have to wear a costume."

"He's not scary."

"He made one of the residents at Garden View scream."

"That's because he surprised her."

Cara sent her a look.

"Okay, I admit that he's not the most…friendly looking man, but he's nice."

"He hardly talks."

"He's a man who likes to listen." She shrugged. "I'd like a chance to get to know him better."

"I wouldn't chance it."

"It's just coffee. He may say 'no' anyway."

Cara nodded. "For your sake, I hope he does."

He didn't and she'd been thrilled, unfortunately, the timing was all wrong because she'd first had to tell him that they were letting him go. She wished she hadn't been tasked with doing her boss's dirty work. Firing Dylan had been difficult and unfair.

"What happened wasn't his fault," Jodi said to her boss Larry Williams as she paced her office. His unexpected visit should have warned her that he wanted her to do something. He rarely showed up at their office with good news. He had comically attractive features, the kind of handsome found in a cartoon character—thick, wavy brown hair, a broad grin that looked like it could sparkle when he smiled and straight nose.

"Doesn't matter," Larry said, running a hand through his hair that fell perfectly back in place. "I want him gone. Pay him enough to make sure he doesn't say anything."

"It would be easier to keep him here and loyal to the company."

"No, it's too late for that. Besides, there's something about him that makes me nervous. And Natalie thinks so too."

That was no surprise. Dylan seemed to have that affect on most people. But getting arrested because he was caught driving a stolen vehicle wasn't his fault. One of the van's they'd bought had been stolen and Natalie should have done a more diligent background check. Dylan had been stopped by the police after making an illegal U-turn and it was while they were running the van's number that it came up as stolen. The client in the van at the time had been so distraught after having to be transferred to another vehicle the family threatened to sue.

Dylan handled the incident without showing any anger and admitted to his illegal turn, which impressed her. It was one mistake. The other clients liked him and he did his job well, and was always on time. There had been no other complaints. He deserved a second chance.

However, Natalie was his daughter and Larry was easily persuaded by what she said. "But Larry I think—"

"This is for the best."

"But why do *I* have to do it?"

"Because you have a way with people, we don't want a scene."

"Are you telling me HR is afraid of him?"

"Just do it with your natural charm. Trust me on this."

She didn't have much of a choice. He was the boss and he made the rules.

Now she wouldn't see him again. If only Dylan had waited to clarify! Had he meant what he'd said? Had he said it at all? She could call him and find out, but he must have left for a reason. If he'd really been interested he would have stayed.

But he was a man of mystery. She'd discovered that when she'd received another emergency call the one day Dylan had been shadowing her. An emergency that hadn't been so easy to solve…

Chapter Three

Three weeks ago…

"Things are going to be a little tense but trust me," she'd told him as she turned onto the tree lined street where the call had originated, the bare branches dark against the grey autumn sky. "I've handled something like this before."

He nodded.

"We don't get calls like this normally so it's more of a personal consideration on my part. I've worked with the family before, the mother uses our services and I have a good relationship with them and told them they could call me any time during these traumatic events."

He nodded again.

She parked in front of the small boxlike house with faded curtains.

"I'm surprised the ambulance hasn't arrived yet," Dylan said getting out of the car. He looked around. "Or maybe they got here before us."

Jodi locked the car and shook her head. "Oh no. It's not that kind of emergency."

"I thought you said you planned to offer support during a traumatic event."

"Yes, it is, in a way," she said, walking up the crumbling pathway lined with neat bushes. "I'm here about Arnold

Fischer. He doesn't want to give up his license although he's had two mishaps and one major accident. His daughter Margery and her brother, Bud, contacted me."

Dylan lifted his brows in surprise but said nothing.

Jodi walked up to the front door and raised her hand to knock. On the other side of the door they could hear shouting, a dog barking and someone crying. She sent him a nervous look. "Do you want to wait in the car?"

He shook his head.

She knocked on the door; the shouting grew louder. Jodi looked at him again. "Are you sure?"

He nodded.

The door swung open and a haggard woman in her mid-fifties dressed in a stylish red blouse and tight jeans opened the door. A yapping terrier circled her heels.

"I'm sorry to bother you like this," Margery said, a strand of light brown hair falling from her ponytail. "Dad's furious and Mom's in tears."

Jodi stepped into the house, careful not to step on the dog that was now yapping and circling around her. "You know I'm not a miracle worker."

"But he trusts you." She turned. "He's in the living room. My brother is trying to talk to him now."

Jodi followed her into the light green room filled with overstuffed furniture that seemed meant for a larger house; an array of black and white photos hung on the wall and lined the fireplace mantle. An older man of about eighty-seven sat with his arms folded, gripping keys in one hand. A man, with the woman's same hair coloring, stood over him while an older woman with a grey bun dressed in a floral sweater sat across from the pair, her head bent, her eyes covered. "We've gone over this and you're upsetting Mom," the standing man said.

"I've been driving before any of you were even born!"

"It's time to call it quit, Pops," Bud said.

"No."

Margery took a hesitant step towards him. "You could have been killed."

"Or killed someone," Bud added.

"Everyone makes mistakes." Arnold pointed at his son in accusation. "Remember that crash you had?"

Bud shook his head and sighed. "I was eighteen."

"Right and did I take the keys away from you?"

"It's different," Bud said, resting his hands on his hips.

"How is it different? I made one mistake."

"It's more than one," Margery said.

Bud sighed. "You're too old."

"I'm not too old," Arnold said. "I'm fit. My doctor says I have the heart of a much younger man."

Jodi stepped forward. "Hi, Mr. Fischer."

His gaze darted between his son and daughter. "Who invited her here?"

"I did," Margery said.

Bud folded his arms. "We both did."

Arnold looked past them and his eyes widened with fear when he spotted Dylan. "Then who's this guy? Are you trying to take me away? Do you think you can lock me up? I'm not going anywhere."

"There's no need to worry, Mr. Fischer," Jodi said. "He's just shadowing me."

Arnold continued to stare at Dylan uncertain. "You're all against me."

"No, we want to help you. You won't lose your freedom. Didn't you like when someone took you and Mrs. Fischer to the movies?"

He folded his arms. "The movie was too loud."

"That's because you refused to adjust your hearing aid," his wife said then buried her face in her hands again.

"We're here to serve you," Jodi said. "To make sure you can still do all that you want to."

"I want to drive."

"It's not safe," Margery said.

"He wants to die," Dylan said.

They all turned to him shocked. Jodi glared at him and mouthed 'Be quiet.'

But he kept his gaze focused on Arnold. "I'm right, aren't I? You'd rather die than give up the keys because that means death to the man you used to be. I can understand that. I say we leave him alone."

"Are you crazy?" Margery said.

He shrugged.

"He could kill someone."

He shrugged again. "If he's comfortable taking that risk who are we to stop him?"

Jodi grabbed his sleeve. "Go and wait in the car."

He didn't move, keeping his gaze on Arnold. "Do you agree?"

"I don't want to hurt anyone," Arnold said in a quiet voice.

"And you're afraid of being a burden."

He hung his head. "Seventy years. I've been behind the wheel for seventy years. It was my first love. My first taste of freedom; the first sign that I was a man and you want to take that away from me?"

"A real man knows his limitations; it takes courage to admit them."

Arnold released a long sigh. "I'm not courageous."

"You don't' have to be. You don't have to admit anything." Dylan studied one of the black and white photos on the wall depicting a bygone war. "Medic?"

Arnold nodded and told him which unit he'd served in.

Jodi stepped closer to see the photo that had taken Dylan's interest. It was a photograph of a young man with a bandage covering one eye, another missing an arm. He continued staring at the photo while he held out his hand. "Do you judge a man by what he can't do or by what he can?"

For a moment silence fell and it was the first time Jodi realized that the dog had stopped barking, but instead sat quietly at Dylan's side. Somehow the chaos and anger that they had entered into had ebbed. She turned her gaze to Arnold, who no longer looked at Dylan with fear, but instead with respect and understanding.

"There's a time for a soldier to stand down," Arnold said, rising to his feet.

Dylan pointed to another photo. "Tell me about this one."

Arnold eagerly spent the next half hour sharing his days during the war, and Jodi saw that he no longer looked as broken as he had before. In her experience, she had learned that often seniors wanted to be remembered and acknowledged for who they had been: The young person who still lived inside them.

Without anyone noticing, Dylan gave her the keys. The company would make arrangements to have the car picked up the next day. All cars turned over to them had to undergo a full inspection to become part of By Your Side or they would be traded or discarded.

On the drive back, Jodi sent glances at Dylan amazed. "How did you do that?"

"What?"

"You calmed the dog, stopped Mrs. Fischer from crying and read the situation in an instant. You gave Mr. Fischer back his dignity while taking something away. You don't look like someone who—" She stopped and bit her lip.

"What?" he said with a note of humor.

"Never mind."

"I know I look mean."

"I wasn't going to say that."

He shrugged, making it clear it didn't matter.

But suddenly everything about him mattered to her. She wanted to know more. She sensed a gentleness and compassion underneath his hard exterior. She didn't see a wedding ring, but some married men didn't wear one.

"Are you married?" She quickly covered her mouth embarrassed that she'd wondered that allowed. "I'm sorry. I didn't mean—"

"No, I'm not. You?"

"No."

She bit her lip. She wouldn't ask him if he was seeing somebody, although she was dying of curiosity, that would be taking things too far. Unless he asked her.

Which he didn't.

She changed the subject but had never been able to look at him the same neutral way again. She remembered the slow, tender way his large hand had slid through the terrier's short white fur, its tail wagging in pleasure; the quick way he grabbed Mr. Fischer's elbow when the older man briefly lost his balance after turning too quickly. And she looked at the hand now, large and strong as it rested on his lap and wondered what else it could do. How it would feel touching or holding her.

Now she'd never know.

Chapter Four

A woman.

He'd nearly blown his cover because of a woman.

Dylan tapped his thumb against the steering wheel as he made his way home under a sky that threatened rain.

Getting fired was one thing, falling for a woman like Jodi was another. It wasn't shaping up to be a good day. *No, but I like you.* He groaned. Telling her that had been out of character. He was usually more detached, more controlled. Instead he'd been reckless and nearly ruined everything. The phone call had been a savior. The moment she left, he bolted. It was the best strategy. She could never know who he really was or, better yet, who his grandmother was.

He glanced at the backseat of his car and saw the empty leash he'd tossed there. It had once belonged to a little mutt called Roscoe who'd he'd taken care of for three years. But he felt as if he'd owned the friendly dog all his life. A dog who seemed to read his moods, who looked like he was always smiling and could make any bad day turn around by picking up his favorite toy—an orange octopus—and placing it on Dylan's lap.

He could blame his strange behavior on having to put Roscoe down, but he knew that was a lousy excuse. He'd said what he'd said because he wanted to. He wanted her to know. He wanted to get it off his chest. He thought it would make him feel better since he'd lied to her all these weeks.

It hadn't helped. But he knew he had to focus on something else. What he would tell his grandmother. He knew she wouldn't like what he had to share.

***

Elena glared at her grandson. "Nothing! You have discovered nothing?"

Dylan sat in front of her in the conference room. He could have sent her the final report, but decided to deliver it to her in person. "I've sent you updates—"

"That were as empty as a beggar's pockets."

He shrugged.

"Don't do that. I hate when you do that."

"I don't know what else to say."

"I sometimes wonder if you're truly an imbecile." She lifted a finger. "And if you shrug I will throw something at you."

He folded his arms.

"I want you to find something useful."

"I can't."

"Why not?"

"I got fired."

"You what?"

"Fired." He cut his hand cross his neck. "The ax."

"Why?"

He shrugged.

She balled up a sheet of paper and threw it at him. "Tell me why?"

"There was a misunderstanding, but it was better this way. Things were getting…uncomfortable."

"Have you lost your mind?"

Briefly. Yes. He drummed his fingers on the arm of his chair.

"When things become tough you fight harder."

With Jodi I was ready to surrender. I don't think you would have liked that.

"You're completely useless."

He leaned forward, resting his chin in his hand. "No, I'm not. I've saved you from wasting your time. I've told you the things you can do to make sure that By Your Side doesn't corner the market. You can create a chasm they will never be able to cross. Don't delude yourself by worrying about what they're doing."

Elena stood and pointed to her chair. "Do you want this seat? Do you think you can run this company better?"

"I was just—"

"I give orders, I don't take them. Especially not from someone who can't do a simple job. Someone who doesn't care about where this company will be in twenty years."

He rubbed his nose. "Are we done?"

"If Flynn's Fleets fails in any way, whether in market share, revenue, anything, I will blame you!"

Dylan stood. "I met someone."

Elena's eyes widened. "What?"

He pushed in his chair and walked towards her. "Someone who for a moment made me not give a damn about you or this business. Someone I wanted to be with." He stopped in front of her and waved her questions away. "Don't worry. I won't see her again. There's no chance of that. I just thought I should warn you." He looked down at her. "You'd better lengthen this leash or you will regret it."

She met his gaze. "What do you want?"

"You know what I want."

"Your mother isn't worth—" She stopped when his gaze darkened. "Promise you'll come back to us."

"No."

"Put your suggestions in writing and I'll see about your mother's investment."

He straightened, pleased. His grandmother had been pulling the purse strings on his mother's money for too long. He wanted his mother afforded a little more freedom and share in the company. "Good." He turned to the door.

"But be careful."

He looked back at her. "Why?"

"Don't let another woman become your weak spot. I will use it to my advantage."

He grinned. "I'd like to see you try."

Chapter Five

Cara looked up surprised when Jodi entered the office. Their office was an open space with three desks and a corner office where the supervisor worked. Cara worked as the receptionist. It wasn't a large office, the owner, Larry Williams, worked in another office down the hall. "I didn't expect to see you back here," she said.

Joyce Dennis shook her head, her curly brown hair, bobbing against her smooth round cheeks. Although she was a few years older than Jodi's thirty-three years, she looked younger. She headed operations and Jodi worked as her assistant. Jodi admired her skills in the office and wished she could emulate Joyce's style, but could only afford to wear the same perfume. "I told you you had nothing to worry about," she said.

Jodi sat at her desk. "What are you two talking about?"

"That guy you had to fire," Cara said.

"What about him?"

"Glad it wasn't me," Joyce said.

"How did he take it?" Cara asked.

"He was fine."

They stared at her unconvinced.

"Really," Jodi said with a bright smile. "It was nothing."

"Larry's lucky," Cara said.

"And doesn't he know it," Joyce added. "You've saved his hide more times than I can count. You should be in that corner office instead of Natalie."

"Not really."

"Hey, without your dyslexia I'd be worried about my job," Joyce said with a laugh. "If you put your mind to it, you could be running this company. You come up with all the ideas she takes credit for."

"It's okay, Natalie knows how to package and sell them to the president."

"A couple of reports," Cara said with a wave. "Big deal. You shouldn't let your dyslexia stop you."

Joyce stood. "I'm getting something from the store, want anything?"

The two women declined. Once she was gone, Jodi looked at Cara and said, "Did you put it on his desk?"

"Yes, just as you asked me to."

Cara had helped Jodi put another plan together. She'd been burned enough to know she couldn't trust Natalie.

One day she did want to be in the corner office. She wanted to be where the real change happened and not just one of the foot soldiers, but she couldn't do that without some help and that kept her options limited.

Nobody knew her secret and she'd keep it that way. She'd gotten farther than most and Larry had given her a chance. If not for him she would have still been a driver, he'd promoted her to the role she now had. A position she'd guard for the rest of her life, as long as she kept her secret safe.

Natalie came into the room holding a bottle of champagne. "Party time. We just closed another major contract with Ravenwood."

Jodi felt her heart constrict. Ravenwood? Her Ravenwood?

"What do you mean?" Cara asked.

"Dad loved my idea so much he immediately put it into action."

"That was Jodi's idea and you know it."

Natalie blinked. "Was it? I noticed a basic draft of a vague idea on my father's desk, but it really wouldn't have gone anywhere if I hadn't fleshed it out." She looked at Jodi. "Besides, you understand the hierarchy of things here. I hope you won't forget that next time."

Jodi gripped her hands into fists, her heart filled with anger. She was the reason Jodi had had to fire Dylan and this was the third idea Natalie had claimed as her own and there was nothing she could do.

Cara jumped to her feet. "You little—"

"I won't," Jodi cut in, not wanting her friend to get into trouble.

Natalie set the champagne bottle on Jodi's desk. "You can enjoy this. It's expensive. I'm leaving early." She sashayed back to her office and closed the door.

"She's always leaving early," Cara said.

Jodi lifted the bottle and studied the label. "She's lucky."

"Are you okay?" Cara asked.

"Don't ask me that now." Jodi set the bottle back down. "If I could punch her I would."

Joyce returned looking sad.

"What is it?" Cara asked.

"I just got a phone call. We've had a cancellation. Mrs. Kwan died."

Chapter Six

Death row.

Jodi tried not to think of it that way as she saw the cage door close behind Gus, a little basset hound. He'd been Mrs. Li Kwan's closest companion for the last seven years of her life, but her family didn't want him and he was an old dog. Jodi didn't have the time to attend the passing of all the clients, but for long time ones like Mrs. Kwan, By Your Side tried to make sure that someone made an appearance. This time it was her turn. Mrs. Kwan's daughter had been so distraught and overwhelmed by her mother's passing that Jodi had offered to take the dog to the animal shelter.

However, leaving him there had been harder than she'd expected.

Jodi watched him being led to one of the cages, his sad little face briefly gazing back at her as he was being led away. If only she had more time. *I hope someone sees how special you are. You deserve a second chance.*

We all deserve a second chance, she thought and her mind briefly drifted to Dylan being fired and what he might have said more than a week ago, but she pushed it away. That chance had passed. She blinked back tears not wanting to think of Gus's uncertain future and walked away.

***

All the lights were on. Jodi sighed with a heavy heart as she parked in front of the large five bedroom colonial she shared with her parents. It was the same house where her mother had once worked as a housekeeper and where they had lived for the past twenty years in the basement apartment as live-in help. Four years ago they'd inherited the property on the condition that they rent the upstairs level and other stipulations that Jodi let their lawyer handle.

She didn't enjoy sharing the house with various strangers, the latest, a woman who barely spoke to her and liked to use as much electricity as was feasible. Thankfully, she was scheduled to leave by the end of the month. Jodi hoped that they could have peace for at least a few weeks before her lawyer, Annette Dobson, who vetted the different residents, told her of a new occupant. The house was located in a prime location only forty-five minutes from DC and Virginia so they always had someone ready to rent the main house.

Twice she'd thought of moving, but she needed to stay close to her parents. For various emotional and health issues, they refused to leave.

Jodi walked into the main house, although she and her parents had a private entrance to the basement, to make sure everything was okay. She did that occasionally to keep an eye on things. Once inside she was glad she had when she heard the faucet running in the kitchen, music playing in another room and something sizzling somewhere, the smell acrid. She found the tenant in front of the TV.

"I smell something burning," she said.

The woman swore then dashed into the kitchen just as the smoke alarm sounded. Jodi made her way to the basement level where she lived. She looked forward to a long soak in the bathtub, but knew she had to visit with her parents first. She found them in the living area. Her mother sat in front of the TV wrapped in her favorite floral patterned housecoat, her hair pulled back in a bun with a deep purple scrunchie that matched the lipstick she'd chosen, which she felt complimented her dark skin. Her father sat next to her reading, his glasses low on his broad nose, a tissue sticking out of the front pocket of his red chambray shirt.

"I'm home," Jodi said, glad that the smell of smoke hadn't reached the basement. Instead the place smelled like her father's favorite banana custard.

"What's that sound?" her father asked, staring up at the ceiling.

"She set off the smoke alarm."

"Again?" he said with a frown.

Her mother held out her hand. "Did you get me what I wanted?"

Jodi placed the carton of cigarettes in her hand. "I wasn't able to get you your regular brand because they were out."

Her mother tossed it on the ground. "But you know I don't want any other brand."

Jodi picked the carton off the ground and placed it beside her. "Mom, you are cutting down anyway."

"But it doesn't taste the same." Her eyes filled with tears. "I waited all day."

"Mom."

"If you were Shelley, she would get them for me."

"Mom, please."

She wiped her tears. "All day I was looking forward to it. I didn't ask for anything else. I asked for only one thing and you couldn't even get it for me."

"Were you able to get the Lore Hardo Bread?" her father asked.

"I'm sorry," Jodi said, "but when I went by the shop they told me that it's discontinued."

Her mother's eyes widened. "What? My favorite bread too?"

"They've got another brand—"

"Don't tell me about another brand. I don't want another brand. I want what I want." She got up and started to pace, shaking her arms and clenching her hands. "What am I going to do? What am I going to do?"

Jodi reached for her. "Mom—"

She snatched her arm away. "No, no, this isn't fair. Why can't you do anything right?"

Her father stood and took her hand. "My darling. Calm down."

"I'm so unhappy," she said sounding miserable. "I waited all day. All day."

He pulled her close and hugged her. He knew how to soothe her in a way Jodi never could no matter how she tried. Within a few moments he got her mother to sit down and apologize then she asked, "How's your sister?"

"Fine," Jodi said.

"It would be nice if she came around every once in a while."

"I know."

"Invite her over for dinner."

I have. She won't come. "I will," Jodi said in the practiced manner she'd used many times before.

"Have you eaten?" her father asked.

"Yes," she lied. She didn't want him to worry about her. "I'll go now."

She decided to call her sister while she filled the bathtub for a long soak.

"They're asking after you," Jodi said once her sister answered.

"So?"

She added some bubbles to the water, filling the air with the scent of strawberry. "They miss you."

"I don't miss them," Shelley said in a flat voice. "I send them money and pictures, that's all they need."

"They raised us."

"No, you raised me not them."

"Shelley."

"What did Mom do this time? You always ask me to come over when you feel guilty about something."

Jodi inwardly cringed remembering her mother's disappointment with the cigarettes. She hated being predictable. "It was just a thought."

She heard a child's voice in the background. "I have to go," her sister said then hung up before Jodi could say goodbye.

Jodi sighed and placed the phone aside and turned off the water. She couldn't blame her sister for keeping her distance. Shelley wanted to have a normal life. One with a father who wasn't sickly; one with a mother who was sensible and mature.

Their parents' union had been an odd match. Their father had been thirty years older than their mother when they fell in love. He'd been socially awkward most of his life and their mother was simple and kind and eager for affection. Their relationship worked for them, but not when it came to rearing children.

She'd learned early that her mother didn't handle change or stress well and when their father, a former engineer, became ill—first with a stroke, then two falls—all the caretaking fell to her. Her mother managed to keep her various jobs—waitress, retail clerk and eventually as a live-in housekeeper—but that was all. The rest of the family household responsibilities—the cooking, cleaning, caretaking and earning extra money—fell on Jodi's capable shoulders. She missed many school days, but her teachers pushed her through—some out of pity, others from apathy.

In the ninth grade, one teacher let her know how most felt about her after she'd received another failing grade. "I get paid whether you remain stupid or not." Jodi dropped out of school and started working fulltime by taking babysitting jobs and she lied about her age and managed to get low wage jobs no one else wanted. When she was of legal age, she worked in a few fast food places until she was able to convince the owner of the house where her mother was the housekeeper to also let her work there.

She helped her mother and added so much efficiency as to how things were run in the house that the owner began to defer to Jodi, instead of her mother, when she wanted something done. But things had still been tough and the money never enough.

Most of her life she'd lived in fear of being taken from her parents, of her father dying, of her sister not doing well. She lived in fear until she'd managed to get the job at By Your Side, after her father had briefly been in one of the rehabilitation centers the company provided transportation for and she'd spoken to one of the drivers and learned they were hiring. That had changed her life.

The schedule worked for her—odd hours, evenings and weekends so that she could take care of her father—and although the money wasn't good at first, her ingenuity and ease with clients quickly got noticed by Larry, who, at the time, was eager to put the new company on solid ground. She shared her ideas and got more responsibilities and a raise. Enough to help support the family, along with her father's disability and retirement. Due to a bad back her mother stopped working seven years ago. Fortunately, her sister got a scholarship and went to college where she majored in Psychology and eventually married a doctor. They had two children.

Jodi felt proud that she'd succeeded in giving her sister a chance for a different life. One that wasn't constantly marked by struggle. But at times, she wondered if she'd ever find that chance for herself. If she'd ever escape being afraid of people discovering her secret and losing everything.

Her parents still depended on her, although she was relieved that at eighty-five her father's health had stabilized—and she couldn't do anything to jeopardize that. But sometimes, at moments when she was alone in her room, she dreamed of a new life. She wanted all her fears and troubles to go away. She wanted to be carefree. She wanted someone to look after her, to worry about her. To care about her.

But she didn't think that day would come. What man would want to take on the burden she carried?

She remembered the sight of her father holding her mother—his gentle words stopping her from another meltdown, rocking her in his arms—and Jodi felt a sadness welling in her heart because no one had ever held her like that. And she wondered if she'd ever feel a love like that.

I like you.

Dylan. She missed him. She wished he'd stayed. She wished she hadn't had to fire him. She wished she hadn't imagined his words, that he'd really said them to her and meant them.

Why him? Why did she have to be attracted to a guy like him?

Jodi squeezed her eyes shut. If only she could forget the first day he'd shadowed her. The gentle way he'd wrapped Mrs. Sherman's sweater around her shoulders when it had fallen to the ground. How he'd helped Mr. Newman select the right wine at the store for his monthly meeting with his buddies. He'd been so patience with Mrs. Tamaka using halting Japanese and making her giggle. He'd listened to Jodi's ideas about the way the company could assist their clients further. Really listened. And his eyes. She missed those frozen lakes that never made her feel cold, but serene. Less alone.

"Why do you do this?" he'd asked her one day in the office after she'd given him his schedule for the day.

No one had ever asked her before and she hesitated then said, "Because of my father. He hated his lack of freedom following his stroke; waiting for the regular medical transport to come. I know how important it is to control your life as much as you can."

She didn't tell him that she'd felt old even when she was young. She'd started taking over some of the household chores by age five—folding clothes, washing dishes, helping her grandmother working on piecemeal projects she took in such as hand painting figurines and attaching eyes to stuffed toys. Her father was never strong and her Jamaican maternal grandmother did her best to support them on her meager wages, but the fridge was usually sparse and there seemed to be more bottles of medicine inside than anything else. When her grandmother passed away when Jodi was eleven, she felt the loss keenly.

Dylan nodded then tapped her desk with his knuckles. "The company is lucky to have you. I hope they know that."

Jodi nodded, her heart in her throat. His compliment meant more than anything Larry could say.

If only his words had been for real. If only he'd felt the attraction too. If only she didn't have to keep her secret and could face Natalie's deception. If only she could be someone else and escape this life.

But she feared she never would.

Chapter Seven

"What did you do?" Cara asked Jodi the following day.

"What do you mean?"

"Natalie's gone."

"What do you mean 'gone'?" Jodi asked, taking a seat behind her desk.

"Fired. Did you tell Larry about the report?"

"No, I haven't said anything."

"Well, something happened and Natalie's gone. Now Joyce has been promoted and is taking her place and Larry wants to see you."

"Why?"

"Maybe so that you can take Joyce's place."

Jodi's heart began to race. "But I can't take Joyce's job."

"Why not? You practically do it already."

"But I'm just her assistant. I can't—"

"You can't let your dyslexia get in your way. First find out what Larry wants."

This couldn't be happening. It was a dream and a nightmare happening at the same time. She was glad Natalie was gone, but taking Joyce's place may expose her secret and she couldn't allow that. She would tell Larry that if he asked. No one could make someone take a promotion they didn't want.

Jodi felt as if she were going to the principal's office as she walked down the hall.

When she was seven years old she remembered being sent to the principal's office because she'd head butted a fellow classmate who'd teased her about her father. *Your dad is as old as a volcano*, he had teased her. Only once, she'd made sure of that, but the words had hurt.

She remembered walking down the long hallway with angry tears burning behind her eyes. She didn't care that she'd given him a bloody nose she'd do it again. She loved her dad and didn't like anyone making fun of him. He was sick and he was older than all the other dads at school. Sometimes she wished he wasn't so tired all the time—at times he seemed older than even some of her friend's grandfathers—but when he wasn't he could make her laugh and he was fun.

She had no reason to be ashamed, but at a time when she wanted to be like the other kids she stood out. Not only because of her father's age, but also because she'd used old-fashioned British-Jamaican words that she picked up from her father and grandmother.

She'd learned to keep herself away from situations that made her feel like a fish out of water. Jodi had the same feeling of defiance and fear as she walked to Larry's office.

She entered Larry's office and spoke before he could. "I see that Natalie's gone and—"

"Sit down."

"I have something to say first. I—"

He looked more unnerved than he usually did. He ran a hand through his hair, but his hair didn't fall as neatly as it usually did. "You can say whatever it is later. This is important and I need you to listen carefully."

She nodded.

"Have I ever made you feel as though you weren't valuable here?"

"Of course not," she said, taking a seat in the soft black chair facing his desk. "Where is this coming from?"

"I just want to make sure that you're happy here."

"I am."

"I've given you lots of options?"

"Yes."

"And you like me as a leader?"

"Yes."

He took a deep breath looking relieved. "Good. Good."

"But I don't—"

"Natalie's gone so you won't have to worry about her anymore. I realize I should have managed her better than I did, but it's all corrected now."

Jodi studied him. "Are you feeling okay?"

"Yes. I wanted you to know that you're now the new operations director. I don't think you'll need an assistant because Cara can help you with other duties. The office was a little crowded anyway."

"But I can't take the job."

"You have to," he said sounding a little panicked. "The company needs you and I can't hire someone right now."

"You don't understand—"

"Of course I'll give you time to adjust, so don't worry. But I didn't call you here just to talk about that. Garden View is hesitant about signing another contract. I need you to seal the deal for us."

"I will, but I really can't take the position that Joyce had."

Larry leaned forward. "Either you take it or leave the company. There's no other position for you."

She couldn't lose her job. But she couldn't be exposed either. She felt as if she were being squeezed in a vise.

"This is a promotion. I thought you'd be happy. You'll get a raise as well."

Jodi plastered on a smile, inwardly screaming.

Chapter Eight

She spent the next several days in a daze. She had to quit. It was better to quit than to have everyone find out she was a fraud. But she needed the money and she liked what she did.

"You're very quiet today," Margery said. The older woman had stopped by the office to give them brownies her mother had made; a way of thanking them for their services and she'd then offered to buy Jodi lunch.

Jodi didn't have much of an appetite but was eager to get out of the office. They now sat in a small American style restaurant among the smell of chili covered hot dogs and French fries smothered with ketchup. "Is something wrong?" Margery asked.

Yes, everything! "No, just thinking."

"Where's that nice young man who was shadowing you several weeks ago?"

Nice young man? "Who?"

"The man who helped you with Dad when you came to our house."

Jodi paused for a moment. Dylan? Was she talking about him? She never thought anyone would describe Dylan as a 'nice young man'. Fierce looking? Yes. Serious? Definitely. But 'nice'? "Oh, he no longer works with us."

"That's a pity. I think he liked you."

"What! You really think so? Did he say something? How could you tell?"

Margery laughed. "I didn't suspect it, Mom did. She said he always asked a lot of questions about you."

"You mean he talked?" Jodi said surprised. She knew he'd been Mrs. Fischer's driver on different occasions but she'd imagined him being the silent type.

"Yes, she said they talked all the time."

"He rarely talked to any of us."

"Maybe he feels more comfortable with people who are older." She grinned. "You like him too, don't you?"

Jodi's face burned. Was it that obvious? "I'm not sure your mother is right. If he really liked me he didn't act like it. Anyway, he's gone now."

"Do you know why he left?"

"It's a private matter. But I'm sure he'll find something else. He was a very good worker."

"He's a good man too; I wish I could have thanked him more for what he did for my dad. Has he worked with seniors before?"

"I don't know much about him."

Margery rummaged in her purse then pulled out a little black book. "Are you ready to fall in love?"

Jodi blinked. "What?"

Margery clicked the top of her pen. "You heard me. Are you ready to fall in love?"

"I guess," Jodi said, stumbling over the words.

"You're not sure?"

"I have other things on my mind right now." *Like trying to keep my job.*

"Love can still find a way to fit in," Margery said, writing some notes in her book.

Jodi looked at the black book. "What are you doing?"

"A shame he's gone. Mom enjoyed him. She'd actually requested him a few times."

Jodi nodded. She remembered the request. As soon as he was trained he'd gotten popular with the "same day" calls, but she'd put him on van duty hoping to give him a more structured schedule and pay and then he'd gotten arrested… She inwardly groaned.

"She said that he didn't even mind when she took Cashew along. What do you think of a man who likes animals?"

"I guess it's a nice trait, but—"

"Yes or no?"

"Yes, but—"

She snapped her black book closed. "That's all I need to know."

"I don't mean to be rude, but I hope you're not trying to set me up with anyone right now. I'm not ready."

"You're ready," Margery said, putting her black book way. "You just don't know it yet."

***

Jodi didn't have much time to think about Margery's statement as she tried her best to learn her new role. She managed to cover two major gaffs with Cara's help and came up with a system that worked for her, but she lived in constant fear of discovery.

Two days later she had to take a client clothes shopping when one of the driver's failed to turn up. She was helping Ms. Rehnquist, a stylish woman of seventy-six, with her three white, red and green shopping bags—new clothes she planned to wear on a Caribbean cruise—when Ms. Rehnquist said, "This dropped out of your purse."

Jodi looked at the elegant envelope. "That can't be mine. Nobody would send something like that to me. It must be yours."

Ms. Rehnquist turned the envelope over. "But it has your name on it." She held it up to her.

Jodi hesitated not wanting to argue. "Okay, I trust you. You can just slip it in my handbag."

"Would you like me to read it for you?"

"I can read it later."

"No, you can't."

Jodi paused feeling suddenly exposed. How did she know?

"I don't mind," Ms. Rehnquist continued, "and I don't have anywhere else to go. Can I open it for you?"

Jodi closed the trunk. "I guess so."

"Is that a yes?"

She nodded.

Ms. Rehnquist sat in the passenger seat while Jodi got in the driver's side.

"Don't start the car," she said. "I can't read while I'm driving," she said.

Jodi turned off the engine and watched in amazement as Ms. Rehnquist grab a letter opener from her purse and swiftly cut open the gold lined envelope. Inside was a handwritten note on expensive parchment paper lined with finely woven lace.

"*You have been personally selected to join The Black Stockings Society*," she read, "*an elite, members-only club that will change your life and help you find the man of your dreams. Guaranteed.*"

"Guaranteed?" Jodi said with a sniff. "Does it really say that?"

"Yes."

"Then it's a scam."

"I haven't finished reading yet."

"I've heard enough." She turned the key in the ignition. "You can throw it away."

"*Dumped?*"

Her hand fell to her lap. "What?"

She pointed to the letter. "That's what it says, Dumped? Have you been dumped?"

"No."

"*Bored?* It says that too," she said when Jodi looked confused. "*Tired of being single? Ready to live dangerously?*"

"It says all that?"

"Yes, are you any of those things?"

She hadn't been dumped. She did feel a little bored. She'd gotten used to being single until she met Dylan. She'd love to end her single days with him. She shook her head. She had to forget him. "What was the last thing it said?"

"Ready to live dangerously?"

No. Her life was risky enough.

"You only have to answer 'yes' to one of those questions."

Jodi bit her lip. "I would like to meet someone someday."

"*Then this is the club for you.*" Ms. Rehnquist pointed to the invitation. "Yes, that's what it says. *Guaranteed results! Submit your application today.*"

Jodi frowned. "There's that word 'guaranteed' again. And if I was selected why would I have to fill out an application?"

"I'll help you fill it out. You don't want to miss this opportunity."

Jodi hesitated.

"The application fee is small."

Her brows shot up. "There's a fee too?" She shook her head. "No way. That's how scams work. You just get a bunch of people to pay a small amount and end up making a fortune."

"I'll pay the fee then."

"No."

"What do you have to lose?"

She was right. But Jodi didn't want to believe in something that might not come true. She'd let herself stop believing years ago.

"Come on," Ms. Rehnquist urged her. "Let me help you." She got a pen. "I'll read out the questions."

Jodi sighed resigned. "Okay."

"*Teacher or student?*"

"What?"

"That's the question."

"But it doesn't make any sense."

"Of course it does. Would you rather be a teacher or a student?"

"Both I guess."

"Choose one. Don't think about it, just say it."

"I'd love to be a teacher for once. I'd love to have knowledge to give to someone. I always feel that I'm the one learning."

She scribbled the answer down. "That's good."

"Don't write all that down."

"Why not? It might help. Okay the next question is: *Long or short?*"

"Long or short what?"

"Just long or short. I suppose it means do you prefer things to be long or short."

Jodi shook her head. "It depends. These questions make no sense."

"Well I suppose since this is for changing your life. Would you want a long affair or a short one?"

Jodi sat back in her seat and drummed her fingers on the steering wheel. "A long one. I would want it to last as long as possible and I don't see why you have to write everything down."

"One day you'll be able to read something like this on your own, for now bear with me. The next question is: *Cats or dogs?*"

"I'll take the dogs. No, the cats. I really like cats. No the dogs. I'd like to go on a walk with a dog."

"Are you sure?"

"Yes."

She asked her a few more questions then said, "Now you have to repeat the oath. Say these words after me, '*As a member of The Black Stockings Society, I swear I will not reveal club secrets, I will accept nothing but the best and I will no longer settle for less.*'" Once Jodi did, she said, "Good. Can you print your name?"

Jodi tried not to feel insulted. Yet, she did. She knew the alphabet and a few words, but not much else. She took the pen and printed her name.

"You can leave the rest to me."

"You'll keep this a secret, right?"

"I always have."

Jodi widened her eyes. "When did you know I couldn't read?"

"Oh," she said with a small laugh. "I thought you were talking about the club."

"You mean you know about them?"

She nodded.

"Are you a member?"

She just smiled then said, "When the package arrives call me so that I can read the instructions. It will have a black circle on it."

"Instructions? You mean there's more?"

"You'll see."

***

A couple of days later, Jodi found herself sitting in Ms. Rehnquist's cozy kitchen, a medium sized package sitting on the square, blue tiled table.

"You haven't opened it yet?" Ms. Rehnquist said surprised.

"You told me to call you first."

"I didn't think you'd be able to resist. Go on. Open it now."

Jodi did and inside the box, encased in a purple satin cloth, were four pairs of different types of stockings. "What's that?" she asked, pointing to a black credit card sized object.

"It's your membership card and it says *Jodi Linda Durant, Member, The Black Stockings Society.*"

"You mean I passed? They accepted me?"

"Yes, congratulations." Ms. Rehnquist set the card aside and picked up a stapled stack of papers. "Now for the fun part." She cleared her throat and read, "*Welcome to The Black Stockings Society. Your first assignment is to take your membership card to your favorite manicurist and request a gold leaf manicure.*"

"Okay, that doesn't sound too hard," Jodi said relieved.

"Following that you'll take your membership card to the Java Juice shop and ask for a Magic Mango Smoothie."

"But I don't like—"

"Just do it."

"Okay, what else?"

"Then it says, *You have to choose a pair of stockings to wear to your reading lessons.*"

Chapter Nine

Jodi stared at her open mouthed. "My what?"

"Reading lessons."

"But I don't have reading lessons."

"You do now. You're to go to the Smith building three days a week at seven o'clock. It says that you must attend for six months or you'll forfeit your membership."

"But I can't."

"The lessons will be discreet and you'll work with an experienced tutor. What is there to be afraid of?"

"I tried it once." She'd tried for three months, almost ten years ago, and still ended up a failure.

"You have to keep trying." Ms. Rehnquist held up the paper. "Decoding these black marks isn't magic, just a skill. With practice you'll be able to do the same."

She wanted it. But she didn't think she could manage to finally accomplish something that scores of teachers hadn't been able to do—teach her how to read.

But if she learned how to read then she wouldn't be exposed in her new position. This chance had come at the perfect time. If she learned to read her secret would be safe forever. "Okay, I'll do it. What else does it say?"

"I don't know."

"What do you mean?"

"The rest is sealed and is meant for you to read on your own." She handed her a closed envelope.

"They wouldn't know if we peeked."

"I think it's important that you're able to read what's next. It will motivate you with your studies. You should be able to read it and understand the basics in about three months."

Jodi sighed and nodded in reluctant agreement. "How do they know so much about me?"

"They do a lot of research on their applicants. It's a privilege."

"Will it really work?"

"All you can do is try. First you have to follow the first instructions."

***

Her manicurist, Tina Park, wasn't so sure. "That's all?" she asked. She wore her advanced years well, her smooth porcelain skin only touched by three birthmarks—one under her eye and two under her right ear-that drove her crazy. She stared at Jodi perplexed. "Are you sure you want the gold leaf manicure?"

"Yes."

"How about a reverse French manicure with glitter?"

"No."

"A hot stone manicure?"

"Next time."

"How about airbrush?"

"No, Tina," Jodi said with a laugh. "Just the gold leaf."

She made a face. "I wanted to have some fun today and it doesn't seem like you."

"I'm trying something new," Jodi said then watched Tina paint her nails a coral color before she used tweezers to attach gold leaf to her nails.

The following day, Jodi parked in the local strip mall where the noisy Java Juice shop sat among a sandwich shop, with one of the sign's letters unlit, and a bank that was closing. She walked into the empty shop, her heels clicking against the yellow tiles, the scent of coconut and raspberry greeting her. She approached the bored looking clerk who was playing a game on his cell phone.

"I'm here to order a Magic Mango smoothie," she said.

He didn't look up. His long dreads shielding the front of his face, the back of his hair was shaved. "We don't have that."

She took out her membership card and put it on the counter. "I was told that you do."

"Nope."

"I have to—"

An older gentleman with a severely short haircut came to the counter. "What seems to be the problem?"

"She wants something we don't have," the clerk said. "The Magic Mango smoothie."

"I'm sorry we don't—" The man paused when he noticed the card on the counter. He whacked the young man on the back of the head.

"Ow!" the younger man cried, rubbing the back of his head. "What was that for?" he asked in an injured tone.

"For not paying attention." He tapped the counter.

The young man looked at the card and softly swore. He put his cell phone down. "I'll—"

"No, I'll take care of this. You come up with five reasons I shouldn't fire you." He smiled at Jodi. "Come with me." He turned and led her to the back through a door that said 'Employees only'. They walked down a few steps and through a long dark hallway.

"Where are we going?" she asked unsure she should continue to follow.

"I don't know."

Jodi blinked, surprised. "You don't know?"

"I'm sorry for the delay. I hope you won't tell them about it." He stopped in front of a dull red door and knocked twice with his knuckles. "Goodbye."

He walked away before she could reply. Before she could follow him, the door opened, filling the dark hall with light. A petite woman wearing dark, four-inch high heels and a tight black suit, stood in front of her with a smile. "Hello, Jodi, I've been expecting you. My name is Doreen."

Jodi entered a room that looked like a replica of her walk-in closet except it boasted large mirrors, a cream settee and chandelier overhead.

"What is this place?"

"A place for you to try on your clothes." Doreen gestured to the row of outfits. "As your personal stylist I hope you'll be pleased by what I've chosen for you."

Jodi looked around the room in awe. "You mean this is all for me?"

"Yes. Isn't it time you dressed for your new role?"

She'd imagined it but never thought it could happen. She only imagined she could wear expensive clothes like Natalie and Joyce. She never had anyone give her this much attention. "But—"

"Membership has its privileges. Come on, let's see how you look." Doreen picked up a top and trousers. "I chose these because I think a statement top and slim trousers will suit your body shape. They will draw attention to your assets."

Jodi didn't care the reason; she wanted to try them all. She loved the soft feel of the bold blue and red silk top, and the elegant cut of the black suede trousers.

She felt like a little girl playing dress up as she tried on a blush pink wrap dress and gold heels, then a striped black and white damask dress with a pair of shiny black boots.

"Is there anything you don't like?"

"No, I love them all. I can't choose."

"You don't have to. I'll have everything delivered."

The word 'delivered' was an understatement. Hours later, a team arrived at her place, emptying out her wardrobe and filling the entire space with her new items.

For her reading lesson Jodi chose a burgundy long sleeve top with a fitted waist and flare sleeves and a mid-thigh black skirt to go with a pair of black lace stockings.

She stared at herself in the mirror amazed. She wanted this new life. This new look. It suited her. She looked like a woman who could run a business, who dated wealthy men, who'd never had to open an empty fridge or see a failure mark on her report card. She looked like a success. She wanted to own this feeling, and feel this way all the time.

But by the time she stood in front of the three-level Smith Building, her confidence had been shaken. Although it wasn't tall it seemed to loom over her and she felt exposed and vulnerable. She was still a fraud. The fancy clothes didn't make her a success. By going through these doors she was admitting that.

However, she had to try. If she didn't want to make a mistake that could cost her her job she had to take this chance. She heard Ms. Rehnquist's voice. *Free lessons with a private tutor, discretion assured. What do you have to lose?*

Her future loomed before her. In six months she would be able to read. Ms. Rehnquist said three but Jodi didn't believe she would learn enough that fast.

Jodi took a deep breath and opened the glass door. She always hated entering new environments because she didn't know what to look for. She couldn't look at the directory and read where the location was. Fortunately, the instructions Ms. Rehnquist had given her said the Resource Center was on the second floor.

She walked up the stairs to the second level that overlooked the first. It looked harmless. She was afraid the Resource Center would be like a library, filled with books. But it had the look of a lounge with round tables, comfortable chairs and polished tiled floors. She took a seat near the window. She clasped her hands together; she was doing the right thing.

She was ready to be daring. Jodi took another deep breath when she heard footsteps coming. This was it. She swallowed then turned when the footsteps stopped. When she saw who stood before her, her chest tightened and her mouth fell open.

Chapter Ten

No. No. No. This was all wrong. She was hallucinating. No, she wasn't hallucinating, she was having a nightmare. A horrific nightmare where a man who looked liked Dylan, dressed in a dark orange sweater and blue jeans, had shown up to teach her.

She closed her eyes then opened them again, expecting him to morph into someone else. He didn't look exactly like Dylan, only resembled him, she tried to convince herself. The Dylan she knew had a goatee; this man was clean shaven. The Dylan she knew didn't wear glasses; this man sported a pair of square dark rimmed frames.

He hesitated then sat down beside her, his leg brushing against hers, sending an electrical shock through her.

He smelled like Dylan, that unmistakable light musky scent that reminded her of white birch, cinnamon and French apple. Her heart began to pound.

"What are you doing here?" he asked in a low voice, although they were alone.

He knew her. That meant it was him. Why did it have to be *him*?

Jodi gripped the strap of her purse. "You first."

He motioned to his bag. "I'm a tutor here, I teach literacy. Are you a new tutor too? I think we might have gotten the schedule mixed up because I booked tonight."

"Yes. No."

"Which one is it?"

"No, I'm not a tutor."

Dylan nodded. "So that must mean…"

Jodi stood. "That I'm in the wrong place," she finished in a clipped voice. "Obviously," she said, forcing a laugh, trying to sound lighthearted. "I made a mistake."

He stood. "You mean you're in the wrong building?"

"Yes, that's exactly what I mean. I'm in the wrong building. Excuse me." She raced down the stairs.

She skidded to a stop at the front entrance where a formidable, dark skinned woman blocked her path. "Go back inside right now," she said.

Jodi looked around, unsure. "You must have me confused with someone else."

"I know who you are, Jodi."

"What?"

"And I know what you're supposed to do. You are to follow instructions. My name is Rania." The attractive full figured woman held up a hand, her gold bracelets clicking together, a large ring on her finger catching the light. "We'll make more formal introductions later. Right now do you still want to be a member of the Society?"

Jodi sent a panicked glance to the second floor. "You don't know what this means. I can't go back up there."

"You haven't answered my question. Do you still want to be a member of the Society?"

She wrung her hands. "Yes, but—"

"Then turn around."

"No, you don't understand."

"Turn. Around."

"I can't be taught by him. Give me another teacher." She pressed her hands together in a plea. "Anyone but him. Please."

Rania rested her hands on her hips unmoved. "He's good."

"I don't care. I can't—"

"Yes, you can. Now go."

"Let me just explain—"

Rania opened the front door. "You are free to go." She held out her other hand. "Just give me your membership card and we'll both forget this ever happened. I'll have someone retrieve the clothes."

"But I already know about your existence."

"You'll have a hard time proving it."

"Knowledge is half the battle."

Rania narrowed her eyes. "Is that a challenge?"

Jodi felt her stomach go into knots. She didn't know enough about them to make such a challenge and she didn't want to fight anyone. "No, I just need you to listen."

"Listen to excuses you've been giving yourself for years?" Rania scoffed. "If it's not one thing it will be another. The time for excuses is over. Either you want this more than anything or you don't."

"I do want it."

"Then get over your pride and walk back upstairs."

Jodi felt tears building. "I just don't want him to know."

Rania rested a hand on her shoulder. "We wouldn't have selected him if we didn't think we could trust him. You can trust him too."

She didn't care about trust. She cared about being ashamed. She looked at Rania and knew she could never understand. She didn't seem like a woman easily persuaded. Jodi blinked back her tears. Maybe she should give up. Maybe she was in over her head. Maybe—

"Do you always want someone taking credit for your ideas?" Rania said. "Do you always want to pretend that you can read the cookbooks you have lined up in your bedroom?"

"How did you—?"

"Do you always want your sister to live the life you wished you could have for yourself? Don't you want to feel the way you look? Because I see a woman with a bright future ahead of her. Don't you want to be that woman?"

"Yes."

Rania closed the front door, satisfied. "That's what I thought." She pushed Jodi towards the stairs. "Then go.

You've wasted enough time already. Remember, what starts off hard becomes easier."

Jodi didn't reply, she gripped the chrome stair railing and reluctantly climbed back upstairs, feeling as if she were walking inside a wind tunnel, the strength of her fear and resistance threatening to push her back. She made it to the top step, took a deep, fortifying breath and went back in.

Chapter Eleven

She found Dylan sitting at one of the tables where he had set out some paper and books. Probably books without pictures, the kind she hated the most. How could she reveal her secret to him? Oh God, why did it have to be him?

He looked up at her. "Still lost?" He looked at his watch. "My student should be here in a minute, but if you tell me where you're headed I can help." He stood.

Jodi collapsed down in front of him like a ragged doll.

He frowned and sat on the edge of the table. "What are you doing?"

She briefly covered her face, then let her hands fall to the table, she kept her gaze lowered.

"Jodi?"

She lifted her eyes to meet his.

Slow dawning crossed his features.

"Go ahead and say it," she said, ready for him to tell her that he'd thought she was smart. How much she'd fooled him.

"How much do you know?"

She paused. She hadn't expected that question. "I know the alphabet and a couple words, but not much."

"Don't worry we'll do an assessment so we can start at the right level. Do you mind if I ask you a couple of questions?"

She folded her arms. "Go ahead."

"How did you get a driver's license?"

"The DMV accommodates non-readers. I had someone read me the written part and then after that my driver's license renews automatically."

"But what about street signs and addresses?"

She held up her cell phone. "GPS helps and maps and if I really get turned around I just ask for directions, but that's why I kept my route routine when I first started, no surprises. Being on call would be a nightmare for me. But I know everywhere now by landmarks and the map in my head."

"The items on the menu at the coffee shop?"

She tapped the side of her head. "With the help of a friend, I memorized it all."

"How do you do your job at the office?"

"I use text-to-speech and a lot of dictation and my friend helps."

"How do you know so much? You spoke to the residents about Chaucer and the Spanish Inquisition. You know about the latest bestsellers and classics. History."

"I like to listen to audiobooks and podcasts. I like to learn, I just never got the chance to learn to read. And in a world of words you learn to adapt." Jodi sighed. "Anymore questions?"

Dylan glanced at the time. "More than we have time for."

"I was being sarcastic."

"Oh."

"Can I ask you a few questions?"

He shrugged. "Sure."

"Why do you look so different?"

He looked down at his clothes. "Do I?"

"Yes, especially the glasses. I never pictured you wearing them."

An unreadable expression came and went. "Anything else?"

She looked at his shirt. "Did you go on a shopping spree or something?"

"Hmm."

She supposed men needed retail therapy too, getting fired was never fun for anyone, but his clothes looked expensive. He had a worker's body, but sitting on the edge of the desk, he commanded the room. He seemed like the kind of man who could make any environment work for him. His casual attire looked as if it could pay for a trip abroad. Perhaps he'd found a discount outlet. She shifted her gaze from his clothes to his eyes surprised to find him studying her in a way that made her skin tingle. "What?"

"You don't need to be angry."

Why hadn't she noticed before how his voice resonated? How the low deep vibration seemed to stir something within her? "Do you want to know the truth?"

He nodded.

"I'm angry at myself. I'm embarrassed, okay? I'll pay you."

He shook his head. "You don't have to pay me."

"I'll pay you to quit."

His brows shot up. "Why would I want to quit?"

"So that I can get another teacher. It's nothing personal. I'm sure you're a great teacher, but I can't…It's a long story."

"No."

"What?"

"I won't quit."

"But I don't want your help."

"Why not?"

"I just don't."

"Is that pride or fear talking?"

"None of your business."

Dylan pulled out a sheet of paper and placed it in front of her. "Let's first assess where you are."

Jodi pushed the paper away. "Didn't you hear what I just said?"

He pushed the paper back and rested a pencil on top of it. "You can take as long as you need."

She snapped the pencil in two and rested the broken pieces on the paper. "You must be loving this. The woman who fired you now needs your help. I don't want to be some pity project."

"I don't pity anyone who's brave enough to admit when they need help.

"You once told me that you wanted to get a promotion and this is a straight way to that. You learn to read and your career could skyrocket and that means a significant increase in salary. On top of that, a number of the ideas you'd told me about could start to be implemented. So you'd have more power."

Was that pride or fear talking? He'd asked her. Her pride had been wounded but she'd been foolish enough to believe she even had half a chance with a man like him. It stung but it was honest. If she pushed her pride aside all that was left was fear.

A big looming fear.

A fear that had always been there, that maybe she was too dumb to read.

"What if..."

He folded his arms and waited.

"What if I fail?" she finished in a quiet voice.

"I don't fail."

"I didn't say you. I said—"

"If you fail then I fail and I don't plan to fail. So what do you say?" he held out his hand.

Jodi looked down at his hand. In six months she'd know how to read. It was the offer of a lifetime. She shook his hand then froze, feeling the heat of his palm, the soft grip of his fingers around hers. She started to pull away. "First, did you…"

He tightened his grasp. "Did I what?"

"Did you mean what you said at the coffee shop?"

"What did I say?"

Jodi briefly shut her eyes. Right, she'd imagined it. She knew it. She released her grasp. "Never mind."

He didn't let go. "If you mean what I mentioned about liking you, yes I meant it." He drew her close, letting his gaze slowly trail the length of her, lingering on her new manicure and lace stockings. "Every word."

She licked her bottom lip, feeling breathless. "Oh."

He released her hand. "Unfortunately."

"Why unfortunately?"

"Because I don't date students," he said in a flat voice.

Her heart fell. "You don't?"

He adjusted his glasses and shook his head.

Her heart lifted as a thought came to her. "Well, if you want—"

"You're not going to quit and I'm not going to quit. We're both going to have to stick this out through the end."

"And then what?"

"And then…we'll see." He winked at her. "Don't worry, Jodi. I'm a patient man."

Chapter Twelve

That was a lie.

Dylan rested his head on his arms in the now empty room, Jodi had been gone five minutes, but he'd been unable to move. He'd been able to be distant and professional the rest of the session with her, but he already felt his stamina fading.

Six months? He couldn't touch that sexy, beautiful woman for six months? He wasn't that patient. But he would have to be. He'd made a promise to the owner of Harrell House and he didn't want to blow it.

"What are you still doing here, Flynn? I have a student coming in ten minutes."

Dylan lifted his head and looked at Nikia Washington, the founder of Harrell House, an older woman with blonde highlights and ruby red lipstick. "What do you do when you meet the right woman at the wrong time?" he asked.

"You cannot date students. That's the rule."

He gathered his items. "I know that."

Nikia lifted his chin, forcing him to look at her. "All those years ago, I took a chance on you. Don't let me down."

"I won't."

"You promised."

"This isn't about—"

"You have to be more guarded. I warned you to make sure that no more clients fall for you."

He held out his arms in surrender. "Do I look like I do it on purpose?"

"I know. That's what makes it worse, but it's bad for business having students fall for you all the time. Twice I had students coming to me in tears when they had to end their sessions with you."

"It's because I'm good."

"No, because you don't know you're appeal. At first you look so…" She shook her head. "I thought it would be safe giving you only male students until…"

Dylan cleared his throat remembering one of his favorite students, Hudson. A thirty-five year old electrician who wanted to get certified. "I really liked him. He was a great guy."

"And he liked you too. So much so that you didn't even realize you'd gone out on several dates with him."

He felt his cheeks burn. "We had a good time."

"Until you found out that he—"

Dylan waved the awkward and painful memory away. "Okay, okay. That's enough." Fortunately, Hudson met someone else and they kept in touch.

"My point is that you're sometimes clueless when it comes to reading people, so you must keep things as distant as possible. You have this strange ability to draw people to you once they get over…" She gestured to him.

"How scary I look," he finished.

"Yes. I don't want to lose you, but you have to tone down your intensity a little. Otherwise I can't let you continue to work with us."

He didn't like the thought of that. Harrell House had been just what he'd needed when he'd gotten in trouble as a teenager, following the death of his father, and been forced to do community service. Harrell House was the one place people didn't expect him to do their dirty work, didn't fear him, and didn't want something from him.

He liked helping people and feeling useful. It wasn't something that happened in his day-to-day life. His grandmother needed him to be someone else, his mother needed him to protect her, his siblings needed him too, but his students just needed him to be there for them. He didn't want to lose something he'd been doing for almost seventeen years. Now at thirty-six he couldn't imagine his life without it.

Unfortunately, Jodi was a threat to that. Just as she had been a threat to him when he was undercover. He had to focus on the goal—teaching her to read. Even if he wanted to be with her, he knew there was no chance for them. She could never find out who he really was.

He would follow the rules and keep his distance. That's what he did best.

Chapter Thirteen

He had never felt like ripping pages out of a book before. He did now. Dylan watched Jodi labor over a passage and gripped his hands in his lap. He glanced out the window at the dusting of unexpected snow on a lamppost outside. It was spring, but the sky hadn't noticed.

He counted to ten, as he listened to her halted and painful reading in the background, then returned his gaze back to her. It didn't help that he couldn't stop watching her mouth move, or notice the way she would cross and uncross her ankles, shifting the position of her dark green skirt against her thighs, which made him wonder about things he shouldn't.

He felt his control and patience thinning. He'd done everything right. He'd been professional, reserved. For nearly four months he'd been helping her, giving her his best and she was not making progress.

She was failing.

He hated failure.

He picked up a pen then slowly set it down afraid he might throw it instead. "You haven't been practicing," he said, cutting her off.

She looked up from the paper, startled. "Yes, I have. I work very hard."

Now she was lying to him, he hated that even more. "It's not showing," he said, making sure to keep his tone even. He didn't want to sound angry, just disappointed. "You should be farther along by now."

"I've done everything you've told me to do."

"If you have then you wouldn't be struggling right now."

She pointed to the children's book. "I'm reading it, aren't I?"

"Barely."

She snapped the book closed. "I'm done."

"Sit down."

Jodi tossed the book on the table. It slid across the surface and fell to the ground. "No, I'm through with this."

Dylan picked up the book and set it slowly down, he kept his voice low. "You have to work harder."

"I do work hard."

"Not hard enough. Based on the assessment we did, I created a personalized schedule for you. There are timely, practical goals to be met and you're not hitting them."

"Maybe because you're a terrible teacher. Maybe because I hate every minute I have to spend with you telling me what I'm doing wrong; what I should know; how far I should be compared to your damn schedule. I'm not a robot. I'm not a test subject." She tapped her chest. "I'm a person and I want this more than you could ever imagine, but you make it worse. You make me feel like a failure. You think I don't feel disappointed? You think it doesn't hurt that I keep making the same mistakes? But it's the look you give me that makes it worse." She grabbed her coat off the back of her chair. "So I'm done." She moved to leave.

He blocked her. "Wait."

"No, I shouldn't have said yes to this. I knew it wouldn't work."

He held out his hand, motioning to her seat. "You need more time. Learning is—"

She pushed his hand away. "Don't you get it? I'm not sick of learning. I'm sick of you." She pulled a note out of her handbag and balled it up. "I was going to give this to you. You're the first person I ever wrote something to in my life, but it doesn't matter anymore." She tossed the scrunched up paper on the table. "You're my worst nightmare. A teacher who doesn't care. You're like all the rest. But don't let that worry you. You didn't fail. I did."

She said something else, but he didn't hear her. Something else kept echoing in his mind.

I'm sick of you. It wasn't the first time he'd heard those words. He'd first heard them from his father when he'd failed his first eye exam. 'You're not trying hard enough. Your eyes are weak because you are.' He'd lost being chosen for student council in a race he hadn't even wanted to enter. 'That's because they know you're not a winner. You have to be the best. You're not working hard enough.

If you're number two you're last. Get out of my sight, I'm sick of you.' His father's words echoed in his mind.

He remembered the time with his grandmother when he'd missed a swing in baseball and she'd turned her back on him. The implication being that if he'd practiced more he wouldn't have failed. It stung and he practiced more. But he never became the best, so he left the sport, even though he loved the game. He'd learned that good enough never was.

He didn't want her to feel as he had as a child. He remembered that lonely, isolating feeling. He knew Jodi. He knew she was smart. Knew she could learn. Instead, he'd thought about the outcome rather than the process. He'd only looked at the goals, and the deadlines and milestones he'd put in place because he liked her and wanted her to succeed. He hadn't put *her* in the equation. But he knew now he had no one to blame but himself. He'd been too hard on her. He'd lost his temper and had said things he shouldn't have.

For a moment he'd become them—his father and grandmother and the thought disgusted him. He *had* been a terrible teacher. It was his job to do better.

He grabbed her wrist before she could leave. "I'm sorry," he said. "You're right. I'll do better."

She shook her head. "It doesn't—"

"Please give me another chance."

"Maybe it's not you and it is me. Maybe I can't learn.

Maybe—"

Dylan took out a pad and wrote down something then handed it to her. "Read it."

Jodi shook her head and sighed. "No."

"Please."

She took a deep breath then sounded out the short sentence. "Yes…you…can." Tears filled her eyes. "You think so?"

"Could you have read that a couple of months ago?"

She looked down.

"I want you to write 'I can do it' ten times. And then read it out loud."

She hesitated.

"I know you don't feel as if you can trust me, but I want this as much as you. I will make sure—"

"It's taking too long. You said so yourself. I should—"

"I was wrong." He lifted up the wadded piece of paper. She reached for it. "No, don't read it."

"Sit down."

She sat and clasped her hands together. "Dylan, please."

"You said it was for me," he said also taking a seat.

"It's stupid. I didn't know what I saying."

He smoothed it out. "Too late now," he said then started to read.

Thank you. You helped me get a dream. I red my first bill today. Thank you again. Jodi.

He briefly held his head in his hands and closed his eyes, feeling the weight of his shame. He'd scolded her because she hadn't progressed on his time schedule. He had grand plans for her. But all she'd wanted to do was read something so simple, so ordinary. Something he'd taken for granted.

She hadn't failed. She'd already accomplished so much. *He* was the one who'd been blind. He opened his eyes and read the note again.

"I told you it was stupid," Jodi said.

He ignored her. He didn't care that she'd confused the word 'red' and 'read' he remembered her frustration with the words 'flower' and 'flour' and how she'd wondered why 'loose' and 'choose' didn't rhyme and why 'off' and 'of' sound so different but 'read' (pronounced: reed) and 'read' (pronounced: red) looked the same but sounded different?

He didn't have an answer, though he was certain there was one. But that didn't matter now. She'd written him four lines. Lines that were like poetry to him. *You're the first person I ever wrote to in my life.* He finally realized how far they'd come. How special this moment was.

Dylan carefully folded the note then wrote a word down on the notepad.

Jodi stared at it stunned. "It's too long."

"Sound it out."

"Mag knife cent."

"Close. Mag nif ee cent." He sounded it out for her. "Magnificent." He tapped the word. "That's you."

"You didn't think so a few minutes ago."

"I said I was wrong." He closed the workbooks. "Tell me what you really want to learn."

"I want to learn to read."

"What do you *want* to learn to read?"

She shook her head.

"Tell me."

"It sounds silly."

"If it's something you want, it's not."

"I want to be able to read a recipe and follow the instructions."

He nodded. "Okay, then that will be one of our goals. And just so you know, you already can read. You're better than before." He wrote down another word. "Read it."

"'Wait'." She looked up at him confused. "Wait?"

He nodded. "That's my problem. I can't do it anymore."

"You can't wait?"

"No."

"Wait for what?"

He wrote something down and pointed.

"You," she read. She paused, then pointed to herself. "Me?"

He nodded.

"You can't wait for me? Why? I don't understand."

He wrote down something else.

"'I want to'?" Jodi read. She looked at him. "You want to what?"

Dylan couldn't stop a smile. "I want to do a lot of things, but that's not what it says. It says 'I want *you*.' Don't guess when you're reading, take your time."

"It's your handwriting."

"It's not my handwriting and you're changing the subject."

"Because I don't know what to say."

"Write it down."

Jodi bit her lip and shook her head. "I don't think I can."

"You can try."

With shaking hands she scribbled something then pushed it to him.

Dylan looked down then tapped the paper. "That's a drawing."

"I know."

"And it's cheating."

"I don't care. Do you understand what it says?"

He shook his head.

She blinked, shocked. "You don't?"

"I just see two stick figures."

"Yes, and they're—"

"Show me."

She paused. "What?"

"I need a demonstration." He stood. "Show me."

She looked around. "I can't show you here."

"Why not?"

"Won't you get into trouble?"

He pulled her close, his gaze holding her still. "I'm already in trouble," he said in a husky whisper then covered her mouth with his.

Chapter Fourteen

She'd expected a kiss, what she got was much more. His lips were like a drug, luring her to a dangerous delight because there was still something about him, a mystery, she hadn't quite solved. But her body didn't care. Her mind whispered its caution but her heart soared into ecstasy. Her lips matched his in passion, her arms snaked around his body, drawing her closer to him, pressing his solid body against hers.

She slipped her hand underneath his sweater, her fingers roaming over the smooth muscles of his back. His skin warm against her fingers. She felt his hot mouth against the column of her neck and sighed with pleasure, his hands sliding down her back and cupping her butt, pressing her closer to him. She obliged, feeling his hard response to her.

He groaned and drew away. "We have to stop."

"You started this," Jodi said, her heart still racing, her body still warm.

Dylan swallowed and nodded. "I know."

"What do we do now?"

He took off his glasses, rubbed his eyes and then put them back on again. He shook his head.

"You don't know?" she guessed.

He shrugged.

She lifted up her picture. "I drew a hug."

The corner of his mouth kicked up in a quick grin. "I told you I couldn't understand it."

She placed the paper down. "And now you're toying with me."

His gaze sharpened. "No."

"But you regret it."

"No."

She hesitated not understanding his strange behavior. He said he liked her, he'd kissed her, but now he looked at her as if he was a doomed man. "Are you married?"

"You asked me that before. No, I'm not married. I'm not seeing anyone. I'm single."

"Then what's the problem? What are you hiding?"

He folded his arms then rested his hands on his hips as if coming to a decision. "Are you free this weekend?"

"No, I have to be at a party."

He nodded. "Okay."

"But I'm free tonight." She waited wondering if he'd turn her down.

"That's good." He gathered his things, looking pleased. "I'll take you somewhere."

***

What he was doing was crazy, but he didn't care. Dylan walked to his car resolute, the feel of the crisp cold air seeming to give him courage. He'd deal with the consequences he'd have to face with Nikia. He just needed to get

Jodi out of his system then he'd tell her the truth. Maybe he'd never have to tell her, his relationships usually didn't last long.

"Dylan!"

He turned around and groaned when he saw Pam Steinberg waving at him. She closed the distance between them in her typical bouncy way like a kid on springs. Her springy reddish brown hair surrounded her face like a cloud, held back by a black headband. "I'm glad I caught you. Nikia told me you'd still be here. I need a favor."

"No."

She batted her pretty green eyes and pushed out her bottom lip. "Please. He's in the car."

"No."

"I realize that losing Roscoe was hard."

"Roscoe?" Jodi said.

"My dog," Dylan explained.

"But you've got a gift," Pam continued.

"It's cold and I'm really busy right now."

"It doesn't look good for this guy. He's at least eight years old with arthritis. He briefly had a home with a lady willing to take him, but then her pet pig bit him."

"A pig bit a dog?" Jodi asked.

"Yes, seems he got too close to her piglets. She bit him hard enough that he needed stitches. The shelter was able to find someone to foster him for a while, but they can't keep him so they called me, but I don't have the space right now and I thought of you."

Dylan opened the door to his backseat and set his bag inside. "Are you finished?"

"He came through surgery like a trooper," Pam continued, her voice as eager as a salesclerk determined to close a sale. "The scar is minimal and he's so sweet." She turned to her van, which had Basset Hound Rescue, written on the side. "You just have to see him." She held up her forefinger. "Just give me one minute." She dashed over to the van.

Dylan looked at Jodi. "Get in the car before she comes back."

"But why is she talking about giving you a dog?" Jodi asked, walking to the passenger side.

"It's not important," he said, getting in the driver's seat and closing the door. "She—"

"Here he is!" Pam said before Jodi could close her side of the car.

Jodi gasped when she saw a familiar sad face. "Gus!" She jumped out of the car and took the dog from Pam. His tail wagged a little then he licked her face. "I don't believe it."

Pam stared at her. "You know him?"

"Yes, he was Mrs. Kwan's dog. I dropped him off at the shelter several months ago."

Pam clapped her hands together with delight. "Then this is fate." She peered into the car and looked at Dylan who still sat in the driver's seat staring straight ahead. "Don't you think?"

He sighed and got out then rested his arms on the hood of the car. "You know what I think." He wrote the word 'No' in the light snowfall on the hood.

"You two could give him such a good home."

"Oh, we're not together," Jodi said. "And I can't take Gus."

Pam looked at Jodi then Dylan then Jodi again and lowered her voice. "I can see that you're very fond of him," she said, scratching Gus behind the ears. "If you want this little guy to have a good home, then convince Dylan to keep him. He's been fostering older dogs for years and he has a way with them. Even the most depressed dog seems to perk up with him."

Jodi turned to Dylan with a hopeful expression.

Dylan looked at her then Pam and straightened, shaking his head. "No, I told you I needed a break."

Jodi held up the dog. "Look at that face. He is so cute."

"No, he's not."

Jodi looked at Gus's sad face. "Okay, he's not, but I've always found dog owners very sexy."

"I already have a dog at home," Dylan said.

"I've always found a man with *two* dogs sexy."

He nodded.

"You have two dogs?" Jodi said surprised.

"Yes, both sweet seniors who are a lot cuter than him."

Jodi lifted one of Gus's paws and waved it. "Three times the charm?"

Dylan stared at the dog for a long moment then sighed and jerked his head towards the car. "Okay."

The two women squealed then collected themselves. "I knew you'd convince him," Pam said while Jodi settled Gus in the backseat. "He's such a softie even though he doesn't look it."

"I know."

Dylan frowned. "Keep talking like that and I'll show you how hard I can be."

"Thanks a million," Pam said. "This gets you off the hook."

"The hook?"

"When I went inside, I saw you two kissing. Don't worry, I won't tell Nikia." She turned, jumped in her van and drove away.

Jodi looked at Dylan, worried. "What do we do?"

"She won't say anything. She knows discretion is everything."

"I think you should take Gus straight home."

"You're bailing out on me?"

"You said you don't date students. It's a rule. I don't want to get into trouble—"

"You won't."

"We can go out another time, we have plenty of time." She looked down at Gus. "Take him home. It's the right thing to do. He looks a little stressed."

"I think that's his natural expression."

"No, he needs a good warm bed."

"So do I." He adjusted his frames and lowered is voice to a coaxing tone. "Care to join me?"

Jodi hesitated, tempted. "Another time."

Dylan looked down at the dog with mock annoyance. "See that? You're already ruining my love life."

Jodi laughed then walked around the car and kissed Dylan on the cheek. "No, I think it's improved."

"Promise?"

"I promise."

"Let me walk you to your car," he said.

"It's right over there," she said, pointing to the sedan parked a few feet away.

"I don't care," he said then began walking beside her.

She stopped at her car, unlocked the door and opened the driver's side. "It's been quite a night."

He nodded.

"If you have any questions about Gus just call me."

"Jodi, I can promise you one thing," he said in a velvet voice, his eyes studying her face. "When I call you, it won't be about a dog."

Chapter Fifteen

Jodi lay awake that night, her mind too filled with joy and wonder to let her sleep. Oh, that kiss! That glorious kiss! And he wanted to see her again.

But what would happen if someone found out about them? Would he get fired? She'd hate to be the reason he got fired again. Perhaps Gus really had come at the right time. If she'd gone out with him tonight who knew where they would have ended up.

She rested her hand behind her head. She may not have ended up alone tonight. They only had two more months to go. Perhaps they should wait. She didn't want another tutor. She only wanted him. All of him.

She wanted him as her teacher and her lover. She wanted him as she'd never wanted anyone before. He made her feel like anything was possible. He made her feel smart. At first she'd been angry and afraid when he'd accused her of not practicing enough, but then he'd asked her forgiveness and said she was…what was that word? Mag-something. But it made her heart leap and then he'd read her letter.

He said she could read. He made it real. She could read. She knew she still had a ways to go, but she was no longer illiterate, something she feared she'd always be. Her efforts had paid off, but she hadn't done it alone. He'd helped her and believed in her.

She'd have to wait three more days before she saw him again. It would feel like eternity. She wasn't sure how she'd be able to focus but that didn't matter. She would find a way.

***

"You got another dog?" Malcolm said when he saw Dylan's new resident sitting by the wall in the kitchen while his other two dogs—a white mutt named Rosie and a mastiff named Merchant—ate, the metal bowls clanging against the floor as they devoured every morsel.

Dylan handed him a beer then closed the refrigerator and sat with him at the kitchen table. "Shut up."

"But I thought you said you weren't getting another one after Roscoe."

He took a swig of his drink then set the bottle down. "Why are you here?"

Malcolm continued to stare at the dog. "He looks depressed. Does he always look like that?"

"I don't have all day."

"Maybe he's married to a bitch." He held up his bottle in a toast. "Brother I understand." He turned to Dylan with a smile.

Dylan didn't smile back. "She's still my sister."

Malcolm sighed. "I know. That's why I'm here. She wants you to attend her friend's party this weekend. You were sent an invitation but didn't reply. She thinks you lost it."

"You could have called."

"I wanted to get out of the house for awhile."

Dylan nodded in understanding. "Which friend?"

"The gorgeous one."

"They're all gorgeous. My sister has a rating system. Which one?"

"The lawyer."

He swore. Annette Dobson *was* gorgeous, brilliant and ruthless. She used her cunning to her advantage, not caring whether her actions benefited her clients or not.

"She likes you."

Dylan shook his head. "No."

"Please."

Dylan tilted his head back as if in pain. "I can't stand that woman." He looked at Malcolm in wonder. "Why would I want to go to her party?"

"Because she likes you. Your grandmother likes her too."

He nodded. "She likes slimy, coldblooded creatures."

"True, but you have to admit Annette looks great in a—"

"No."

Malcolm pressed his hands together. "For the sake of peace in my home, I beg you."

Dylan swallowed his beer.

Malcolm pushed back his chair as if to stand, the sudden sound of the chair scraping against the floor caught the dogs' attention. They briefly looked at him before they resumed eating. "Do I have to get on my knees? It's just one night."

"What do I get out of it?"

"My undying thanks."

Dylan waited, clasping his hands behind his head.

Malcolm sighed. "It was worth a shot. Okay, you do this and I'll return the favor. I'll be in your debt. I'll do whatever you ask me to do."

Dylan nodded. "Fine, but you'd better be prepared for the day I come to collect."

Chapter Sixteen

Although she hadn't officially been invited to Annette's party, celebrating an important contract she'd finalized, Jodi wanted to look her best, choosing a pair of stripped black stockings and a navy blue wrap dress. She glanced out the kitchen window. The weather had also seemed to want to appear in its finest, dressing the trimmed grass and willow trees in green elegance, the bright sun warming the air, making everyone forget the light snowfall from a few days ago.

It wasn't the first time Annette had asked Jodi if she could use the spacious main level of Jodi's house and back garden to host an intimate 'soiree' as she liked to call it. She usually had a reason why she couldn't use her own place—workers were redoing the kitchen, the landscaper hadn't come in weeks, the bathroom was a mess—and Jodi didn't mind helping out. Even when the last caterer backed out at the last minute and she had to make a dinner for ten. It had been such a hit that Annette had asked her again to assist the caterer by making dessert and some appetizers.

Jodi was in such a good mood she didn't mind the work as she looked over her efforts—Jamaican banana fritters, and avocado and orange salad, but she was most proud of her lime tart with coconut crust. Fortunately, she didn't have to do anything else. She left the kitchen and walked out into the spring air, seeing the well dressed guests enjoying the food feeling a sense of pride. Months ago she would have hidden in the kitchen, but in her new clothes she felt as if she belonged. She only wished Dylan could be there with her.

Annette seemed just as eager about someone showing up. Minutes ago while in the kitchen, Jodi had overheard Annette talking to one of the guests.

"Don't worry," she'd heard a woman say. "Malcolm said he'll be here."

"He's missing the best part," Annette said.

"He likes to make an entrance."

Jodi didn't like to hear Annette unhappy and hoped that her expected guest would soon arrive. Jodi went to the basement to quickly check on her parents then made her way back upstairs. She was in the main hallway when she saw the front door open and Dylan stepped inside.

She blinked, not sure if she was dreaming. She'd wanted him to be here, but this was unreal, like an aberration. But as he got closer she knew it was him in a dark suit, his glasses gone, his face a hard mask.

She opened her mouth to greet him but he looked right past her as if she were invisible. "You don't know me," he said, continuing his march down the hall.

"It's about time you got here," a friend of Annette's said.

She didn't turn to look at him enter the main area, her mind racing with questions. Why shouldn't she know him? What was he doing here? Did he know Annette?

For the next half hour she tried to pretend not to notice him, although it was hard seeing Annette wrapping her arm around his and toting him around as if he were her favorite toy. Or something more. Were they together? Was he cheating? He'd said he was single, but was that a lie?

No, a man who helped people learn how to read and fostered elderly dogs wouldn't be like that. There had to be a reason for this.

Jodi dashed into another room just to get away from seeing him and to cool her growing suspicions. She crashed into someone coming out. She stumbled back and looked up at a man so good looking that for a moment she was speechless. She knew him from somewhere. "I'm sorry."

"No, this is just my luck," he said with a smile. "I wanted to talk to you."

"Me?"

"Yes, about your delicious banana fritters."

She smiled. "Thank you."

"What did you use?"

She told him the simple ingredients and then he asked her other questions before, to her surprise, he helped her forget Dylan and made her feel like one of the most interesting women in the room.

He seemed familiar to her, but she wasn't sure why. "Have we met before?"

"No. I don't believe I've had the pleasure." He held out his hand. "I'm Malcolm Falconer by the way."

"With Flynn Fleet's," Jodi said instantly making the connection.

"The one and only. I'm always looking for ways to treat our employees when we host parties for them and I know your banana fritters would be a hit."

"I'm not a caterer," she said, feeling suddenly shy. "I just did it to help Annette as a friend."

He lifted a brow. "What does it take to become a friend of yours?"

Jodi laughed at his flirtatious tone. "A lot."

He pulled out his card. "If you change your mind."

A striking woman in a plum purple dress came up behind him. "About what?" she asked, giving Jodi the once over.

"My wife," the man said, his natural good mood seeming to fade a bit.

"Gwen," she said, shaking the tips of Jodi's fingers.

"Jodi."

"She's a friend of Annette's," Malcolm said.

The woman's gaze sharpened. "Really? I thought I knew all of Annette's friends."

"No," Jodi said quickly not wanting her to misunderstand. "More like acquaintances."

"I was just complimenting her about the food," Malcolm said. "Have you tried the banana fritters?"

"Why would I? They're fattening."

He winked at Jodi. "And delicious."

"Excuse us," Gwen said, taking Malcolm's arm in a clearly possessive gesture.

Jodi nodded and watched them join another couple, wondering why Gwen would even consider her a threat.

***

"Have you seen where your brother has disappeared to?" Annette said when she found Gwen standing alone on the back patio.

Gwen sipped her watermelon sangria as she stared at Jodi who was talking to one of the wait staff, the cool liquid calming her burning thoughts. "Who is that woman?"

Annette followed her friend's gaze. "Nobody."

"She's very attractive."

Annette shrugged. "In a simple way."

"She said she's a friend of yours."

"I'm her lawyer," Annette said with a laugh. "But she's grateful for the help I give her. She's some assistant at By Your Side."

"And her name is——?"

Annette looked at her friend surprise. "Does it matter?"

Gwen kept her gaze on Jodi.

"You can't be serious. She's no threat."

"I saw Malcolm talking to her."

"He's probably being friendly. She's truly a nobody."

Gwen took another sip of her drink. "I don't care."

"Her name is Jodi Durant and she's as naïve as a child. You don't have to worry about her."

Gwen didn't respond. When it came to her husband and other women, she was always worried.

Chapter Seventeen

She felt a gaze as heavy as a fist.

Jodi turned and saw Gwen glaring at her, not understanding the other woman's animosity. Although Annette and Malcolm had made her feel welcome, his wife, Gwen, branded her an outsider and she felt it even more keenly now.

Jodi went back inside ready to head back to the basement. She'd spent enough time playing make-believe; it was time to go back where she belonged. She saw Dylan in the hall coming from the opposite direction, but looked away and opened the basement door.

"Keep going and don't look back," he said behind her.

She did as she was told and made her way down the stairs then turned to him once they reached the landing.

"What are you doing here?" she asked, but the remainder of her words was smothered by a kiss.

"You look beautiful," he whispered against her lips, pulling her into the circle of his arms. "I couldn't stop thinking about you and now here you are. Am I dreaming?"

She wrapped her arms around his neck, savoring the gentle assault, realizing how much she'd missed him and how it had hurt when he'd looked right through her. "I hope this is real."

He buried his face in her neck. "You smell good too," he said, his breath hot against her skin. "You feel even better." He held her close. "I can't believe I got dumped for a dog."

"How is Gus?"

He slid his hand down her back. "If I knew you'd be here I would have come sooner."

She stopped his hand from roaming lower and placed it back on her waist. "But why are you here?"

He briefly rested his forehead against hers before he straightened and looked down at her. "You first."

"I was—" she began but the look in his eyes, a kind of controlled mischief, reminded her of someone she couldn't quite place. Until the image of a striking, cold woman came to her mind. "Did you know that the owner of Flynn's Fleets is here with his wife?"

"He's not the owner."

"What?"

Dylan waved his hand. "Nothing. What else do you know?"

She frowned. "What do you mean?"

"Why are you here? Who invited you?"

"I wasn't really invited. I just helped Annette with some of the food."

His brows shot up. "You work for her?"

"No, I'm just helping out."

"And you were coming down here to get more wine or something?"

"No," Jodi said with a laugh. "I live here."

Dylan released her and took a step back, shocked. "This is your house?"

"Sort of. It's a long story," she said, waving a dismissive hand. "Now your turn. Are you seeing Annette?"

For a moment he looked ill. "No. Never have, never will."

"But you know her."

"My sister knows her." He rubbed his chin looking unsure. "There's something I should tell you. I'm with Flynn."

Jodi tenderly cupped the side of his face. "Is that why you wanted me to pretend I didn't know you? Did you think I'd be upset because you went to work for our rival?" She took both of his hands in hers and smiled up at him. "Of course not. I'm happy for you." She slid her thumb and forefinger down the lining of his jacket, the expensive material soft against her fingers. "I mean, you must have really made an impression on them to be invited to a function where the president of the company is." She lowered her voice. "And I know that the clothes make the man, but I've noticed you've really been spending a lot lately. You didn't dress like this when you worked with us. Did you come into some money?"

Dylan pinched the bridge of his nose. "It's a little more complicated than that."

"Then what—"

"Jodi, is that you!" her mother called out.

"Yes, Mom. I'm—"

"One of the light bulbs is dead in the bathroom and my TV remote won't work."

"It's probably the batteries."

"Where are they?"

"Never mind," she called back. "Be right there." She looked at Dylan. "Just give me a minute, okay?"

He followed her to the closet. "Who's that?"

"My mom," she said, getting a light bulb from the top shelf. "My parents live in a room down the hall. As you can see, the basement is a separate apartment. We share the kitchen and the living room." She went into the bathroom.

He took the bulb from her. "I'll do this for you. You go change the batteries in the remote."

"Thanks."

She hurried and got some replacements then changed the batteries. "Mom, I told you where the extras are. When you see the warning image in the corner of the screen you just pop them in."

"I didn't see it."

"Where's Dad?"

"Taking a nap. You know after he eats a big lunch he gets sleepy."

"Did you like the food? I made it."

Her mother focused on the TV screen, having lost interest in her. "It was nice."

Jodi looked up and saw Dylan. Since her mother's favorite show was on she knew it was best not to introduce him now. She walked over to him and led him to her bedroom. "I hope you don't mind but my mother has her routines and she gets upset when they get changed. I'll introduce you next time." She gestured to her bed. "You look a little tense. Sit down."

He stood at the door and folded his arms. "What is going on?"

"What do you mean?"

"How do you know Annette?"

"She's my lawyer."

Dylan stared at her astonished. "She's your *what?*"

"My lawyer, what's wrong with you?"

"How can that…" He took a deep breath. "I'm sorry." He took off his jacket, resting it over a chair and undid the top button of his shirt. "Start from the beginning."

"There's really not much to say. I met her when I inherited this house. She was very helpful reading and explaining everything to me when I told her about my 'dyslexia' and my parents couldn't be bothered, so she was a great champion with all that needed to be done."

He hung his head for a moment then looked at her and said in a low voice, "But if you inherited the house why are you and your parents living in the basement?"

"It's part of the will. I get to stay here with my parents as long as we leave the main house free for renters, but right now it's empty, which is odd."

He undid the buttons on his sleeves. "And where does the money go?"

"Money?"

"From the renters."

"Oh, Annette handles that. She says she has to take care of maintenance, utilities, property taxes and such. It pays for all of that. It is a large house. She's generous really. My parents and I used to work for the former owner and didn't know all that went into the particulars of managing this property."

He briefly closed his eyes and nodded, rolling up his sleeves. "I see. And the party?"

"Party?"

"Why are you helping her with the party?"

"I only help sometimes when she's in a crisis. I don't mind. It only happens a couple times a year so it's not too tiring…and what are you doing? You look like you're getting ready to fight."

Dylan softly swore and looked down at his sleeves. "Sorry, you're right," he said and then pulled them back down.

Jodi ran her hand over the bedcovers, wondering why he didn't want to join her. "Are you sure you don't want to sit down?"

"Hmm."

"What's wrong?"

He walked over to her dresser and looked at her row of hardcover cookbooks—some tall and slender others thick and square.

"I love the pictures in them," she said, his strange silence making her uneasy.

He pulled one of the books off the dresser and turned its spine to face her. "And what does it say?"

She shifted. "I don't—"

"Yes, you do. Take your time."

"Um…Easy and Fast…Cooking."

He slid the book back in place. "Good."

She felt the tightening in her chest ease. "The pictures inside are really amazing. I look at some before I go to bed."

He nodded. "And one day you want to follow one of the recipes." He turned to her. "And make me something delicious."

She smiled. "Yes, did you like the lime tart?"

"I don't like lime."

"What do you like?" She waved a finger when he sent her a knowing look. "And don't say 'you'."

"Why not? It's true."

"At least he liked my banana fritters," she muttered.

"Who?"

"Mr. Flynn."

He frowned, confused. "Mr. Flynn?"

"Yes, the face of Flynn's Fleets."

"You mean Falconer? Malcolm Falconer?"

She nodded. "That's right, the owner of Flynn's Fleets."

"I told you he's not the owner. He's the president. My grand…understanding of the business is that."

"It doesn't matter. He liked my food."

"I'm sure I'll like it too, but I ate before I got here. I didn't plan to stay long."

"And wanted me to cook for one of their events." She pulled out his business card. "He even gave me this."

Dylan snatched the card and tucked it inside his trouser pocket. "I'll keep it safe for you." Before she could protest he said, "I expect you to make a special batch of banana fritters just for me."

"Only if you're taking good care of Gus."

"He's living like a king." Dylan looked around the room. "I want to see the will."

"The original is with the attorney."

"But you should have a copy." When she hesitated, he smiled. "Don't you trust your boyfriend?"

"No, it's not that. I don't have it."

His smile fell. "Of course."

Jodi bit her lip wondering if he was unhappy with her reliance on Annette. "She's taken good care of us. She said it was hard to set everything up because I wasn't able to do it myself. She didn't charge extra or anything. She's been really kind to me. My parents trust me and I trust her and…you're doing it again. Why do you keep rolling up your sleeves like that? Are you hot?"

He scratched his chin. "Hmm."

"Well, cut it out. It makes you look like a thug."

He folded his arms. "Sorry."

She smiled at him and softened her tone not wanting him to be upset with her scolding. "I was just as surprised about the will as you are. This house is enormous, but I can't afford to lose it. Moving is out of the question. My mother doesn't take change well."

"You're not going to lose the house. I just want to read the conditions and make sure everything is in order."

"I don't have it."

Dylan ran a hand down his face.

"What's that expression for?"

He let his hand fall and shook his head. "Nothing." He picked up his jacket. "Are you going back to the party?"

"No." Jodi leaned back with a smile of invitation. "If you wanted to spend a little more time I'm—"

Dylan put on his jacket. "Good," he said as if she hadn't spoken. "Because I have a feelings the party is about to end."

Chapter Eighteen

"You said you wanted to see me alone?" Annette said, closing the door to the study behind her, her reflection staring back at her in the large window across the room. She rested against the dark oak door and turned to Dylan, who stood in front of her. "You're looking fierce." She lightly touched his chest. "It looks good on you."

He placed a hand against the door, his arm next to her head. "You think so?"

"It's very sexy."

"You're not afraid?"

"I like a little danger."

He nodded. "I'm glad because somebody's been a bad girl."

"You finally noticed?" she said, trailing a finger along his jaw.

He slowly blinked.

"And you're here to punish me?"

He nodded again. "I met the owner of this house and she told me about the will."

Her eyes widened in shock. "Why would Jodi tell you—?"

He lifted her chin. "How should I punish this bad girl?"

Annette held his gaze, trembling at his touch. "I'm sure Jodi didn't explain everything."

"That's what I thought. So I asked her to let me read the will, but she doesn't have a copy. Why is that?"

"She trusts me to handle everything. I've taken good care of her and—"

Dylan pushed away from the door, disgust in his voice. "You don't take care of anyone but yourself. You'd steal milk from a puppy."

Annette clicked her tongue. "Ouch, that's a bit harsh. I like puppies."

"I forgot, it's people you can't stand."

"Only stupid ones."

"Jodi isn't stupid."

Annette took a seat and crossed her legs looking bored. "Then you don't know her very well."

"So you admit—"

She feigned a look of innocence. "I admit nothing." She smoothed down her skirt annoyed. "What's this obsession you and Gwen have about this woman?"

His tone sharpened. "Gwen asked about her?"

"She saw Jodi talking to Malcolm. We both know she's a little paranoid."

He nodded. "She gets it from me. I sometimes get this feeling that there are people out to hurt the people I care about."

She straightened. "Who is Jodi to you?"

"And this crazy feeling comes over me and I feel I have to do something. Something that will destroy the threat."

She surged to her feet. "Dylan, this isn't funny."

"And I start to wonder what I should do first. Should I be swift or slow? What's the perfect revenge?"

"I don't know what she told you, but—"

"I want the will."

"It's a private matter."

"I can make it public."

"Is that a threat?"

Dylan rested his hands on his hips and flashed a cruel smile. "Do I look like the kind of man who makes threats?"

Annette sighed, her gaze sweeping over him in longing disappointment. "Why do you have to be so sexy?"

He waited.

She folded her arms. "How much time do I have to fix this?"

"Depends on how much you've made."

Her arms fell to her sides. "I don't have that money anymore."

"You'll find it. You have three days."

"I need more than three days."

"In three days you're going to call Jodi and tell her that there's been a mistake and you'll take care of it."

"I don't see how any of this is your business."

"Three days. Make it right or I will come after you."

Chapter Nineteen

Joyce looked outside with a groan as large drops of rain pounded against the office window. "Damn spring."

"The rain is good for us," Jodi said.

"But I have a date. He's picking me up any minute and I'll get soaked."

"You can borrow my coat," Jodi said, motioning to her bright pink raincoat, which hung on the coat rack. "It has a hood."

Joyce smiled and grabbed it. "Thank you! You're a lifesaver. I'll pay you back." She dashed out the door.

"Now you'll get soaked," Cara said.

"Nope. I have a huge umbrella and I'm glad I could help." Jodi said, putting her things away in her desk. "I wonder who she's seeing. She's been really happy these last few months."

"All I know is that he drives an expensive car," Cara said. "Speaking of expensive, you still haven't told me about that outlet place where you got all your new clothes."

"I told you, it was just a lucky find. It's now out of business."

"And you're seeing someone."

She hadn't told her about Dylan yet. She knew she had to keep her membership in the Black Stockings Society a secret, but the reading lessons and her new relationship were also things she wanted to keep guarded. Especially when there were still so many questions. Why hadn't he wanted to stay with her a little longer? He'd practically raced out of her bedroom. "Yes, but it's not really anything yet."

She remembered getting a phone call from Ms. Rehnquist two nights ago. She'd been alone in her bedroom still reeling from Dylan's strange behavior at the party, and then having him alone in her room when her phone rang. "Have you read the instructions yet?" she asked.

Jodi paused. "What instructions?"

"From the Society."

She felt embarrassed. Over the last several months she'd forgotten about her membership. "No, I haven't read them yet." She scrambled and looked inside her closet where she'd put the box with the two remaining stockings and the sealed instructions. "When do you want me to come over?"

"I told you, it's for you to read now. I just wanted to remind you."

"But what if I—"

The connection went dead. Jodi took the box and set it on her bed. There was a sealed envelope that said 'For Jodi' her heart began to race again as she recognized the words. *You can read now*, Dylan had told her. She had to believe that. She could read. Even her job had become easier as she recognized words that had once seemed foreign to her.

She took a deep breath. Four months ago this would have been impossible, but she could do this now. She broke the seal and opened the remainder of the instructions.

Choose a pair of stockings to cook in.

She frowned then read it again. That's all? That was easy. She read the next line.

Then make a meal for someone special.

She smiled. That was also easy. She would love to make something for Dylan. Her eyes went to the last line.

From a recipe you read.

Jodi paused then slowly read the instructions again. Not just any recipe, but one she could read. That shouldn't be too hard now. She'd read these instructions all by herself hadn't she? She jumped off her bed and grabbed one of the cookbooks, her heart pounding. Yes, this would be something she could do.

However, when she looked at one of the recipes, her heart sank. There were still too many words she didn't know or understand. She shoved the book back in place in disgust. Why would they ask her to do something like this? Why couldn't they ask her to follow a cooking show? It would probably take her another month or two to be good enough to recognize all the terms.

"Are you seeing him tonight?" Cara asked, breaking into her thoughts.

"No," she said. But she'd seen him last night for her reading lesson. She'd been more determined than ever to learn the words she needed. She'd bought one of her favorite cookbooks on desserts with her to her lesson and pointed out words for him to describe like 'concentrated' and 'granular' and 'distinctive flavor' until he stopped her.

"Jodi, I know how important this is to you, but this book is advanced and you're not at this level yet."

"But I have to be."

"You'll get there, but trying to push yourself you'll only end up frustrated. I can give you several words to practice if you like."

She sighed, defeated. "Okay, but could you read a few more words for me? She turned a page and pointed. "Like what does that say?"

"Luxurious velvety chocolate."

She flipped to another page. "And this?"

"Creamy coffee buttercream."

She motioned to a few lines below it. "And what about this?"

"Swirled chocolate and luscious—" He snapped the book closed. "I'm done."

"Why did you stop? What did it say?"

"I'll tell you next time. Let's switch to another topic."

She smiled. "Those pictures are mouth watering, aren't they? Was it making you hungry?"

His eyes caught and held hers. "Yes, but not for what you think."

Heat crept into her cheeks, a delightful shiver running through her, and soon the words she could recognize sprang to her mind like 'moist' and 'intense' and 'heat'. At that moment she felt all three. And for the first time she only cared about one thing—learning everything about him. She looked at his eyes, wondering what he liked to watch; she studied his lips wondering what he liked to eat. She looked at his shoulders, wondering what he did on the weekends.

"You're not making this easy," Dylan said in a deep tone.

"I'm not?"

He shook his head. "Not when you keep looking at me like that."

Jodi lowered her gaze and swallowed, fighting to tap down her attraction. "I'm sorry."

He released a long sigh. "Me too. Whatever you feel, I feel it more."

She stared at him startled.

He frowned. "Why do you look so surprised?"

"It's just that…"

"What?"

"The day of Annette's party, when you were in my bedroom, you didn't seem…" She searched for words.

"Interested?"

She nodded.

"I had something else on my mind."

"Can I ask what?"

He folded his arms on the table. "You'll find out soon."

"You can't tell me now?"

"No," he said with a smile. "It's a surprise."

And to her annoyance he didn't say anything more, but he promised her a surprise this week so she looked forward to their next session to find out what it was.

"No, actually my lawyer called," Jodi said, answering Cara's question. "I have to go to her office. She said it was something urgent."

Chapter Twenty

Annette had always been sweet to Jodi, but the woman who greeted her that evening had all the charm of a sour grapefruit. Jodi opened her mouth to ask her what was wrong when she realized they weren't alone.

Dylan rose from a chair, which had been obscured by the door. "Surprise."

"What's going on?" Jodi asked.

Dylan waited.

Annette sighed. "There seems to have been a mistake with the will."

Jodi sat down sending Dylan a nervous glance. What was he doing there? Had he said something to her? Was she going to lose the house? "A mistake?"

"Yes, the house goes to you."

"I know that," Jodi said confused. "We went over all the conditions."

Dylan took a seat but didn't speak.

Annette stared at him for a long moment then turned to Jodi. "There are no conditions."

"No, conditions?"

"No." She clasped her hands together and lowered her voice with all the sincerity of a disgraced politician at a press conference. "I admit that I've made a mistake. I went over the will again and noticed my error. I can no longer be your lawyer and I hope that this will compensate you." She lifted a check off the desk and handed it to her.

Dylan took it before Jodi could and read the amount. He crumbled it in his fist. "Try again."

"You bastard."

He blinked, bored.

She turned her wrath to Jodi. "I thought you trusted me. I thought we had a good relationship. How could you go behind my back to a shark like Dylan Flynn and—"

"I didn't," Jodi said, pained by the accusation. "It's just that we—" She stopped before she admitted that they were seeing each other. "I don't know what he said, but—"

"Annette," Dylan cut in in a sing-songy voice. "You're starting to make me angry."

She glared at him.

He didn't blink.

Jodi looked at the two perplexed then stood. "Annette, I'm sorry. I don't know what's going on. Dylan, let's go."

He didn't look at her, his gaze fixed on Annette. "If she walks out that door, you know what I will do."

Jodi spun to him. "Are you threatening her?" She looked at Annette. "Did he threaten you?"

Dylan opened his fist and stared at the crumpled check in his hand. "Did I?"

"No," Annette said. "Please sit down." She wrote another check then held it up for them both to see. She shot Dylan an ugly look. "Is that better?"

"Only if you hand it over with a smile."

She curled her lip.

He took the check. "I suppose that's the best you can do." He handed the check to Jodi. "Here you go."

She stared at the amount and shook her head. "I don't understand what's going on."

Dylan stood. "I'll explain later."

"It was an honest mistake," Annette said. "I hope that you can find it in your heart to forgive me."

Dylan opened the door. "Let the church say 'Amen'."

Annette flashed him a crude gesture.

***

"What just happened?" Jodi asked Dylan as they rode the elevator down to the main floor.

"Annette is a fraud. She used your…trust to fool you and convince you that you needed her firm, but the will said that you got the house and could do with it whatever you wanted." He nodded to her purse. "You didn't have to rent out to anyone and that's to pay for the money she made."

"But why would she do that?"

"Because she tests the air with her tongue."

"What?"

"She's a snake."

"All this time she was tricking me?"

"It's okay, it could happen to anyone."

"Not anyone," Jodi said in a bitter tone. "It couldn't happen to someone who could read."

"You can read now," Dylan said, stepping out of the elevator. "Don't feel bad. People of all types can get swindled. Just be happy it's over."

"You know you didn't really tell me how you know Annette."

He held open the front door for her. "She's a friend of my sister."

"Was your sister at the party?"

He nodded. "Yes, you met her and her husband, Malcolm Falconer."

Jodi stopped. "She's your sister?"

He nodded again.

"But then…wait…why did Annette call you Dylan Flynn not Rodgers?"

He sighed. "Because that's my name."

"And you now work at Flynn's Fleets?"

"I don't work there."

"But you said—"

"I'm the grandson of the founder. My grandmother runs the company."

"I don't understand. Then why were you working at By Your Side?"

"I went undercover to see how it was doing."

"You mean you went to spy to steal ideas?" Jodi stared at him as if seeing a stranger. She'd trusted him, shown him parts of the company, shared ideas they'd planned to implement. He could use that information and help their biggest rival. He'd seemed interested and now she knew why. "You're no better than Annette. You used me. You abused my trust."

"Jodi."

She marched to her car. She'd been betrayed by two people she'd trusted. "I don't want to have anything to do with you."

"I didn't tell them anything. And if it will make you feel any better, my grandmother didn't talk to me for weeks."

She opened her car door. "I don't care. I thought you were better than this. But you're no better than a criminal."

"I'm pretty sure it's not criminal to spy on your own company."

She stopped and stared at him. "What? You own By Your Side?"

He nodded.

"But Larry Williams—"

"Works for me. Several years ago I thought my grandmother could use a little competition." He shook his head. "No, that's not right. At first I had something to prove, then I realized I enjoyed it."

Slowly everything fell into place. "I told you about Natalie stealing my ideas and Larry covering for her."

He nodded.

"And you're the reason Natalie was fired and Joyce and I got promotions."

He nodded again. "I meant it when I said I hope you know how appreciated you are."

"Then why were you fired?"

"I asked Larry to do that. I knew it was time to leave and make some changes."

"And why did he ask me to do it?"

Dylan smiled. "Can't you guess?"

Jodi shook her head.

"I wanted to see you one last time." He winked. "Still mad at me?"

"How can I be mad when you changed my life? Although, it was scary at first."

"I know. When I found out your secret I was a little worried, but I would have made sure the position was held until you were ready."

She leaned against the car and stared up at him, squinting against the bright sun behind him. "I still can't believe it."

"I need you to keep my secret. I don't want anyone else to know the truth."

Jodi playfully narrowed her eyes. "I knew you were hiding something. Do you have any more secrets?"

He shook his head. "You?"

Only an exclusive club that I can't tell you about. "No."

"Good. Now let's take this relationship to the next level. Are you free this weekend?"

"Yes."

"Good, because I want to treat you to dinner."

Chapter Twenty-one

He treated her to a lot more than dinner.

Jodi shifted her gaze over the three people in front of her—two she'd already met before—the attractive woman with the cold eyes and the handsome man by her side—and another individual who seemed friendly, a round faced cutie who spoke so softly at times she had to strain to hear him.

They sat together in the elegant Spanish restaurant. She knew the pair was Dylan's sister and brother-in-law and now knew that the younger man was his brother Josh. She just wished he'd given her more of a warning. He'd only told her his plan when they arrived at the restaurant and said, "Oh, they got here before us," as the maitre d showed them to their seats.

"Who?" Jodi asked, taking off her raincoat, which had protected her from the light drizzle outside.

"Gwen, Malcolm and my brother Josh."

Jodi looked at him with wide eyes. "They're here?"

"Yes, I wanted them to formerly meet you."

"Why didn't you tell me? Meeting your family is a big step." She looked down at her dress. "I should have worn—"

"You look beautiful and I didn't tell you because you may have said 'no'."

"I would have definitely said 'no'. Your sister—"

"But since you've already met them it shouldn't be too awkward. And Josh likes anybody."

"But your sister—"

"Now smile and wave, they're looking at us."

And now Jodi was looking down at a menu she couldn't read. Only the word 'Menu' seemed to register in her mind. Was she so nervous that she'd forgotten how to read? Was it because she was completely out of her element? She felt as if at any moment someone would put a spotlight on her and expose her as a fraud. What business did she have dating the owner of the company where she worked? And how could she try to pretend she had anything in common with a man like Malcolm who was the face of Flynn's Fleets? She couldn't talk about banana fritters all evening.

"Are you ready to order?" the waiter asked.

Josh opened his mouth to reply, but Malcolm beat him to it.

"Not yet," he said to Jodi's relief.

"He always takes forever to decide," Gwen said.

"I'll give you a few more minutes," the waiter said then left.

Jodi scanned the menu. Perhaps she should just give up and have whatever Dylan ordered. That was usually what she did when she went out to eat with others.

Dylan gently nudged her with his elbow and said in a low voice. "You look anxious. What's the matter?"

"The menu. I can't…" She didn't want to say 'read it'.

Dylan looked at her menu then frowned. "Did the maitre d give that to you?"

"No, your sister—"

He snatched it away. "It's in Spanish," he said, glaring at Gwen.

She giggled. "I'm surprised it took her so long to notice. Don't look at me like that. It was a little harmless fun."

Dylan nodded then said something in Spanish to her that she didn't find funny at all before he returned his attention back to Jodi. "You can look at my menu. I know what I want."

"His last girlfriend spoke three languages." Gwen lifted one shoulder in a shrug. "I guess a man's standards can't always be high."

Dylan narrowed his eyes; Malcolm shot his wife a look.

"Actually, that was *my* girlfriend," Josh said in a soft voice.

"Was it?" Gwen said with little interest.

Jodi continued to study the menu not daring to look up.

"Try the *plancha*-grilled calamari," Josh said, "you won't be disappointed."

"Don't be mean," Gwen said. "I doubt she knows what 'plancha' means."

Dylan lifted a brow. "She doesn't need to know what it means to enjoy the food."

"*Plancha* is basically a metal or cast iron plate," Josh said. "And the calamari is doused in lemon. It's delicious."

Jodi smiled at him. "Sounds good."

"But what will you have it with?" Gwen asked.

Jodi gripped the menu unsure.

"I could order for you if…" Josh stopped and looked at his brother for how to proceed. Dylan gave a subtle nod. "You'd like," he finished.

Jodi closed the menu. "Yes, please."

And she wasn't disappointed when the food arrived. She loved Josh's selection, but the dinner went downhill from there. Malcolm and Josh tried to keep the conversation light, while Gwen continued to make pointed catty remarks, and Jodi tried her best to shrug them off until Dylan set his knife and fork down and said, "One."

They all looked at him startled, then Gwen said with a nervous laugh. "What are you doing?"

"Two."

"Dylan, you don't really think that I would—"

"Three."

Jodi touched his sleeve. "What are you doing?"

He kept his hard gaze on his sister. "Four."

"It was a silly game we used to play as children," Josh said, his gaze darting between his siblings. "Dylan used to have a terrible temper when he was younger so our mother taught him to count to ten."

"Five."

"And it was supposed to calm him down. But sometimes he didn't."

"Six."

Gwen held up her hands. "Okay, okay. I'm done."

He waved at her. "Goodbye."

"But I haven't finished eating," she said.

"Seven."

Malcolm stood. "We'd better go."

Gwen snatched her arm away and opened her mouth to say something.

Dylan held up his hand in warning. "Say one word and I'll jump to ten."

She grabbed her purse and stormed away. Malcolm made his apologizes then followed.

Josh sighed. "Does this mean no dessert?"

"I'll send you two deliveries on me," Dylan said.

His brother smiled and stood. "It was nice meeting you Jodi."

"Same."

He left.

Dylan lifted his utensils and began eating again.

Jodi watched them leave the restaurant then turned back to him. "Well your sister hates me."

"She doesn't hate you; she's just…that way. But she was extra moody today. I'm sorry."

Jodi playfully hit him on the arm. "That's what you get for not warning me."

"It wouldn't have made a difference. Did you like Josh?"

"Of course I liked him. What's not to like?"

He scooped up some rice, looking pleased.

"What did Gwen think would happen if you reached ten?"

He smiled, but didn't respond.

"Dylan, you have to tell me. What was she afraid you would do?"

"Someone's been asking about you."

Jodi paused, adjusting to the change in topic. "Me?"

He nodded.

"Who?"

"Gus. Would you like to see him?"

"I'd love to, but first tell me what—"

"I'll tell you another time." He gave her a light kiss then said, "Now finish up, Gus is waiting."

Chapter Twenty-two

"What is wrong with you?" Malcolm demanded once he and Gwen were alone in the car.

"Nothing."

"If you didn't want to come you should have said something."

"I wanted to get him back for upsetting my friend."

"Annette can take care of herself. And why take it out on Jodi? Why did you have to pick on her like that?"

"What's the big deal? I don't understand why he's seeing her anyway. Does he really think we'd have anything in common with her?"

"She's funny."

"So is a seal."

He glanced at her then back at the road. "That's nasty even for you."

"I saw you looking at her."

He rolled his eyes. "Not that again."

"You think she's pretty."

"I think she's beautiful." When his wife looked at him astonished he said, "Do you expect me to lie?"

"She's not beautiful. Don't exaggerate. You just said that to make me angry."

"You're already angry."

"I'm not angry, I'm annoyed."

Malcolm shook his head. "I can't believe we're having this conversation."

"You were flirting with her."

"I wasn't flirting."

"You're interested."

"Not in that way."

Gwen watched a car speed past them. "I wish I could believe you."

"Are you crazy? Do you think I'm dumb enough to hit on Dylan's woman?"

"I think you're smart enough for him not to know. My brother can be dense sometimes."

Malcolm turned on some reggaeton music. "You don't know what you're talking about."

"Turn that off."

"No."

"I saw you two looking cozy at Annette's party as if you've met before."

"I don't know her."

She clicked the music off. "You gave her your card."

He pounded the steering wheel. "Because I liked her banana fritters!" Silence fell between them. Malcolm shook his head in regret. "There's nothing more to it. I realize I made a mistake once. I told you I was sorry."

Gwen turned to look out the window, welcoming the silence in the car.

She hated reggaeton music but she hated his lies even more. The bastard thought he was so clever. Did he really think he could fool her? He used to be more discreet, but now he was getting sloppy. She didn't like sloppy. She knew he was seeing someone from By Your Side. It was his way. But Jodi Durant had surprised her. She wasn't his usual type, but maybe he was changing with age.

She had proof of what he was up to—the phone calls, the notes with her initials in his phone. And Jodi even had the gall to wear the same raincoat she'd worn the night Gwen had followed them from the office. She'd had her head covered then. But Gwen had seen them kissing in the car. *This* car. Brazenly. And now this woman was going to make a fool out of her brother. She would take her time, she wouldn't strike yet, but she would not see her brother get hurt.

***

Malcolm sat on the side of his four-poster bed, the lights dim. He rested his head in his hands. He didn't know what had gotten into her. Gwen could be rude and moody, but she'd never been like this before. He liked to stay on Dylan's good side because his brother-in-law always proved useful. Navigating the Flynn clan was always a test of wills.

He glanced down when his cell phone rang. He noticed the number then looked towards the bathroom door where he heard Gwen showering. He quietly walked into the hallway and answered.

"I won't be able to see you tomorrow," he said. "I have to deal with a situation."

"Do you think she's getting suspicious?" his lover asked.

Yes. "You don't need to worry about anything."

"Are you sure?"

He saw the door open down the hall and his five year old daughter came out rubbing her eyes. "Give me some time," he said in a low voice. He covered the phone then said, "Can't sleep?"

His daughter shook her head.

"Malcolm?" he heard his lover say.

He silently swore wishing she'd know when to be quiet. "Go back to bed, baby," he told his daughter. "I'll be right there to tuck you in. Okay?"

She smiled and nodded then disappeared back into her room.

His lover's voice grew more insistent. "Are you still there?"

"Yes," he said, keeping his voice low.

"When will you leave her?"

"You know I have to wait for the right time." He opened his bedroom door and realized the shower had stopped. Gwen would be out soon and expect to see him in bed, plus he had to go see his daughter.

"I just want to be with you," his lover said.

"I have to go."

"I love you," she said.

"I love you too," he replied, although he didn't mean it. He knew it was what kept her in line. He had two women in his life and he had to handle them both well or he could lose it all.

Chapter Twenty-three

Gus was smiling.

Jodi almost couldn't believe it. He still had a hangdog expression, but he looked happy when he and his two companions came to greet her in the foyer of Dylan's sandstone, contemporary style house. She knelt down to pet him.

"Oh my goodness, Gus. Look at you!" she said pleased to see his uplifted demeanor and wagging tail. "And hello," she said, petting the other two dogs.

"That's Rosie and Merchant." Dylan said.

"It's a pleasure to meet you both." Jodi stood and the happy trio walked down the hall and into another room. "You really are a miracle worker," she said.

"It doesn't take much," he said, leading her into the living room. "Would you like anything to drink?"

She shook her head and took a seat on the grey custom sectional, sinking comfortably into the cushions. "I'm stuffed. Thanks." She glanced around at the faux-finished smoke colored walls surprised that the color gave the room a warm feeling rather than a cold one.

"I have a patio. We could sit there and—"

"I'm so comfortable I don't feel like moving." She sighed. "I wish my place felt like this. Even though I know the house is mine now, it doesn't feel that way. I've moved some things to the main level, but my parents still prefer the basement."

"You could sell it."

She shook her head. "No, I told you that my mother doesn't like change." She closed her eyes and rested her head back. "I see why Gus is so happy. It's so peaceful here. I feel like all my worries are chased away. I wish I could stay here."

"You can."

She opened her eyes and stared at him. "I wasn't inviting myself."

"I know," he said in a deep, smooth tone. "I'm inviting you to stay the night."

She glanced at the three dogs. "What will the children think?"

"They'll be fine." He pulled her to her feet. "And I won't let you use them as an excuse this time."

Her heart jolted at the heated look in his eyes. "It wasn't an excuse," she said, trying to keep her voice from shaking. "I was worried about Gus's wellbeing."

"As you can see he's fine now."

"Yes." She swallowed feeling suddenly breathless. "You've taken good care of him."

He swept her into his arms. "Now let me take good care of you."

She wrapped her arms around his neck, anticipation making her heart race. "It's about time."

And time was what he took. Dylan didn't do anything fast. He took his time taking off her clothes one item at a time; pulling down the bed sheets and drawing her close. He was in no rush as he explored her breasts, her thighs and her center—first with his fingers then with his tongue—the warm, wet tip causing her to writhe in ecstasy, her body melting into a liquid heat, causing her to tighten.

"Careful," he said with a deep, laugh. "You nearly took my head off,"

"Sorry."

"Don't apologize," he said before reaching for something beside his bed. "Give me a minute to take care of something."

"Need help?" she asked as he opened a condom packet.

He shook his head and quickly covered himself before he pushed her legs apart. "Are you ready for me?"

"I've been ready."

"Sorry to make you wait," he said. He slowly slid inside her. "I'll make it worth it. Go ahead."

She looked up at him alarmed. "What?"

A quick grin touched his mouth. "You can tighten around me now."

Which she did, welcoming him deeper inside her, his hard body hot against her skin. And for the first time in her life she didn't feel like an outsider. She didn't feel like it was the first time with him, she felt a recognition, a long-lasting bond, as if she'd been waiting for him all her life.

"You make me feel at home," Jodi breathed, "like I'm exactly where I'm supposed to be."

Dylan kissed her then said, "Because it's true. You're meant to be with me."

And he showed her how much, hoping she would feel the same about him. Hoping that as he felt the tips of her fingers skim across his back that she wanted to hold him as tight as he wanted to hold her. Possession hadn't been his goal, he'd meant only to persuade her that he was her man. But as her soft sighs mingled with the sound of shifting sheets, the sweet scent of her apple spiced lotion drifted towards him, and a raw feeling of possession gripped him.

His desire for her aroused his hunger for more and he feared he could never get enough.

"Don't leave me," he whispered in a soft voice he'd never used before.

Jodi looked up at him. "I won't," she said and then she smiled, a smile that wrapped him in a warmth he'd never known, one he wanted to hold forever and within seconds he was lost.

***

"Could you do me a favor," Jodi said a little shy. She leaned back against him as she smoothed down the hair on his arm, which he had wrapped around her waist. They lay in bed together in the dimly lit room.

"What?"

"Call me 'Honey'."

"Honey?"

"Yes, I've always wanted someone to call me that. You know, something sweet."

He slid his hand down her leg. "Why not 'Syrup'?"

She playfully nudged him in the chest. "That's not the same."

He pressed his lips behind her ear. "I could call you 'Sugar' or 'Strawberry'."

"Dylan."

"Or 'Tangerine'. Or 'Peaches'. No wait, 'Honeysuckle'." He drew her close and gently squeezed one of her breasts. "I love honeysuckle."

"Just call me 'Honey'."

He toyed with one hard nipple, his voice husky. "Nice, round and juicy."

"That's honeydew." She turned to face him. "I said call me 'Honey'."

He grinned. "I'll try to remember."

"And what should I call you?"

"You know what to call me."

"I'll call you Dee."

He shook his head. "I don't like nicknames. If you want me to answer, you'll call me by my given name."

She drew the shape of a heart on his chest.

"That's cheating."

"I know."

"Write something."

She flattened her hand on his chest. "I don't know what to write."

"You can write my name."

She hesitated.

Dylan closed his eyes. "Go on."

Jodi began then flopped back on the bed. "This is so stupid. I can't even spell my boyfriend's name."

"You haven't even tried." He grabbed her hand and placed it on his chest. "Come on."

She wrote 'Dillan'.

"Close."

"But wrong," she said with a sigh.

He rested on his elbow and began to draw on her stomach. "You got the d right, but my name doesn't have the little man," he said referring to how she remembered the lowercased 'i', "it has the kite," he said writing a 'y'. "And only one 'l' then an 'a' and 'n'. Five simple letters."

"Let me call you Dee."

"No."

"Big Dee?"

"No."

She lifted the blanket and looked at his penis. "Little Dee?"

He snatched the sheet away and covered himself. "Absolutely not."

"I wasn't referring to its size or anything."

"I don't care."

She reached for the sheets. "You're very well proportioned."

He pushed her hand away. "I don't want a nickname."

"Come on. I want to give you a special name."

He stood and pulled on his underwear.

"Are you angry with me?" she asked, watching him tug on a pair of jeans.

"No, you just reminded me of something." He left the room then came back moments later holding a slender, square, brown wrapped object.

"I got you something."

She unwrapped it. "A kid's cookbook?"

"Yes, I want you to make me something special."

"But—"

"The recipes are simple you can do it."

Jodi flipped through the pages then hung her head thinking of the more detailed and expensive versions at her place. She thought of the instructions from the Black Stockings Society. She doubted they meant her to wear stockings making something like 'happy faced pancakes'. She set the book down and pushed it away.

Dylan looked at the book then her, confused. "What's wrong?"

"Doesn't it embarrass you?"

"What?"

"Shouldn't your girlfriend be making you something impressive like Swedish crepes or tiramisu?"

He wrapped his arms around her. "I don't care what my girlfriend makes, as long as she makes it just for me."

"I'm ashamed though. I almost felt as if your sister knew."

"She didn't know. Nobody does and you can read. You're not who you were four months ago. And in time you'll be even better than now. But you have to start where you are. You wanted to read a recipe." He held the book out to her. "Here is your chance."

Jodi wiped away a tear of frustration and disappointment. If he didn't mind, why should she? And he'd taken the time to buy the book for her; it wasn't kind to reject it. "Okay, can I come over next weekend and cook you something?"

He nodded, placing a light kiss on her shoulder. "I'll be waiting."

Chapter Twenty-four

He wished he'd bought her a cookbook sooner.

Dylan watched Jodi as she stood at his kitchen counter chopping vegetables, thinking of everything but food. She wore shorts and a fitted top but it was her stockings that caught his attention. They seemed to shimmer in the light, accenting her thighs, the shape of her calves.

"You don't have to watch me," she said.

"Yes, I do," Dylan said, resting his chin in his hand. "I'm supervising."

She tossed him a look over her shoulder. "You're just staring. I can feel it."

"I can't help it."

"It's making me nervous. Go."

"But—"

Jodi pointed to the door with her knife. "Go."

Dylan sighed and stood. "Come on, Gus."

"The dog can stay."

"That isn't fair," he said, wounded.

"He can keep me company."

"I'll keep you company."

"You're a distraction. Go."

He pointed at the dog. "Don't look so smug. I get to sleep with her."

Jodi picked up a red bell pepper slice and threw it at him. Dylan ducked and laughed while Gus snatched up the food. She more than made up for his dismissal from the kitchen when she presented him with a bubbling hot primavera skillet pizza. Dylan took a slice, the mozzarella cheese pulling as he did so. He took a bite then nodded.

"Delicious, what are you going to make me next?"

"I just made you this."

"I like looking to the future."

She got the cookbook and placed it next to him. "You choose."

He randomly opened it and pointed. "This."

Jodi saw what he had pointed to and sighed. "You would choose the one recipe with a lot of ingredients."

He winked. "Then we'll have to go shopping."

She hadn't thought shopping with him would be fun, but it was. She was used to shopping alone; having to think about her parents' needs and how to stretch the budget, but with him she had no such concerns. Whatever she needed he tossed in the cart and it was nice to travel down the aisle with someone special by her side.

He also made their outing part of her reading lesson, pointing to signs and asking her to read them to him, gently correcting her when she got them wrong.

He picked up cans and boxes and pointed out words. Soon her confidence increased and she didn't care about making mistakes, looking for words every chance she got and she soon surpassed his weekly reading goals for her. On his fridge he used magnetic letters to spell out new words for her to read.

Finally, Jodi brought her cookbooks over to his place and, at first, started reading recipes to the dogs, who liked to lie at her feet while Dylan was out on one of his evening jogs. She soon progressed to reading them short stories.

Over the next several weeks she was at his place every weekend, so often that he gave her an extra set of keys. Jodi kept herself busy shopping and preparing a different meal and she became more confident with both her reading skills and cooking, advancing from the children's book to her adult versions.

She prepared a meal for his brother Josh and mother Adelaide, who seemed to blossom under Jodi's attention. She introduced him to her parents over a meal of stuffed peppers her mother wasn't overly enthusiastic about, but Dylan and her father asked for seconds.

Fortunately, both her parents liked him immediately. "It's a shame Shelley couldn't be here too," her father said.

Jodi continued eating not knowing what to say. She'd made the invitation but her sister had refused and she still remembered her disappointment.

"I'm seeing someone," she'd told her over the phone, "and I'd love you to meet him."

"Great," Shelley said. "When?"

"I'm having him over for dinner."

She paused then said, "I'm not eating with them."

"Shelley, please."

"No, Mom always makes a fuss. I can't take it."

"Just for a couple of hours. I'm not going to host him in the basement, but in the main house. Remember that large table in the dining room? I'm going to—"

"You can have him come over here."

"They're not monsters you know." When her sister didn't reply, she continued. "I want you to meet, Dylan. The invitation's open when you're ready."

"Thanks," Shelley said before she disconnected.

The sound of the dead connection still rung in her ears as Jodi's parents gushed over Shelley's accomplishments.

"Her wedding was so beautiful," her mother said.

"She's our other daughter," her father added.

"The smart one."

"Both of our daughters are smart," her father said.

"Yes," her mother agreed. "In their own way, but our Shelley is super smart."

"Our Jodi is the pretty one."

"Like me," her mother said with a giggle.

Her father kissed her. "Exactly."

"I like everything about Jodi," Dylan said. "I couldn't pick just one thing."

After dessert—strawberries and cream—Jodi took him on a tour of the house. She watched him as he looked around at the pictures on the walls in the tidy family room, the vivid blues of the furniture contrasted with the seashell white on the walls. He frowned. "Where are pictures of you?"

"Me?"

"Yes, funny little baby pictures of you as a skinny kid."

"I was never a skinny kid."

"You know what I mean."

"I don't have any." She pointed to a picture of her parents with Shelley at Shelley's high school graduation. She looked miserable but her parents beamed. "I took most of these pictures. It was a hard time back then, but I still wanted to save memories."

He nodded.

"I don't regret it. I'm really happy for my sister."

"I'd like to meet her."

Jodi turned to him and smiled relieved. "And she'd love to meet you too and…what's that look for?"

"I'm trying to picture you as a kid. You must have been adorable."

She fluttered her eyes. "Naturally."

"And lonely."

Her face fell. "Why would you say that?"

He shrugged. "Just a feeling."

"I had my parents and my sister."

"And I had a grandmother, mother and two siblings and I felt lonely all the time." His gaze held hers. "Until I met you." He gathered her into his arms, enveloping her in a feeling of home.

"I feel the same," she said with a smile, feeling safe in his embrace. "I can't wait for Shelley to meet you."

***

Shelley wasn't what he'd expected. When Dylan finally got to meet her he was surprised by how similar she was to Jodi. They shared the same coloring and bright warm smile. For a moment he was as tongue tied as when he first met Jodi. She introduced her husband, Calvin, and elder son, Brian, who looked about six and stared at him with a look of paralyzed fear.

Dylan was about to say something to assure the boy when he felt a hard object slam against his leg. He glanced down and saw a little boy of about four.

"I'm a ram!" the boy said, his bright brown eyes shining up at him.

"You know better than that," his mother scolded him then looked at Dylan. "I'm sorry."

"It's okay," Dylan said.

Shelley looked at the boy. "Now apologize to—"

"Big Dee," Jodi said with a smirk.

Dylan glared at her.

Her smile widened.

"Big Dee, huh?" Calvin gave him a friendly slap on the back. "The name suits you."

Dylan shook his head. "But it's not—"

"I'm sorry," the boy said and then took his hand. "You can sit next to me Big Dee."

"I'll get you for this," Dylan told Jodi in a low voice of warning, before he allowed the child to lead him away.

As the meal progressed Brian warmed up to Dylan and told him about his favorite show and shared the titles of his favorite books.

"I'm really good," he said. "I read to my brother all the time."

"I can read too," Paul said.

"No, you can't."

"Can too."

"Not as good as me." He looked at Dylan. "Can I read to you?" He jumped from his chair. "I'll be right back."

Shelley began to call after him then Paul said, "Me too," and raced out of the room.

"You don't have to listen if you don't want to," Shelley said.

"I don't mind," Dylan said.

Calvin shook his head. "You might regret it."

"He loves reading," Jodi said. "And he's a good teacher too."

Shelley looked at Dylan surprised. "You're a teacher? I thought you were in business."

"I meant that he's patient," Jodi said with a nervous laugh. "He's taught me that."

Brian and Paul came back holding their books.

"I'm ready, Big Dee," Brian said.

"Me too," Paul added.

Brian sent his brother a look. "Rams don't read."

"Do too."

Shelley motioned to the other room. "If you fight, Big Dee will leave."

Dylan raised his forefinger. "Actually Big Dee isn't my nick—"

"Now go and take him into the family room," Shelley continued in a stern voice, "and remember to use your inside voice."

Both boys reached for him—one grabbing his hand, the other his trouser leg. "Come on, Big Dee," they said.

Dylan managed to send Jodi one last glare; she bit her lip to keep from laughing.

Later she took a picture of him on the ground with the boys—Brian sitting beside him reading and Paul standing and looking over his shoulder. She sent him the photo with the caption *I love reading.*

Dylan stared at the image now, which he'd saved to his cell phone, as he sat in his living room, Rosie staring at something outside the window, Merchant asleep, his right paw twitching, and Gus curled up on the seat cushion next to him. As he studied the image he realized he wanted more moments like this, but next time he wanted Jodi in the picture beside him. He no longer wanted her to be the one left out.

He wanted to marry her; he wanted to give Brian and Paul cousins to play with. Dylan glanced around the room a little surprised by the depth of his desire. He wanted to add pictures of them on the wall. He wanted to get her away from her parents and out of that house. There was something sad and suffocating about it. She belonged with him. She fit into his life perfectly and he didn't like only having her stay on the weekends. He wanted to wake up to her every morning and hold her hand while walking the dogs on warm summer evenings.

He felt a renewed urgency. The tutoring sessions had ended and he'd managed to keep his relationship safe from Nikia, but that didn't make him feel secure. The dinner with Gwen had gone bad and he knew he still had to deal with one major person. He didn't know if Jodi would be able to handle the pressure.

A week later, that person made her presence known.

Chapter Twenty-five

Dylan raced through the front door, taking off his sweaty shirt after a long jog, a little surprised when his dogs didn't come and greet him as they usually did. He called out to Jodi as he headed for the stairs, "Sorry I'm late, Honeysuckle. I just need to change and then we'll…" His words died away when he smelled a particular scent in the air—orange blossoms.

He followed it to the living room and found his grandmother sitting alone. He looked outside the window at the driveway and softly swore; if he'd been paying closer attention he wouldn't have confused his grandmother's black Lexus with Jodi's Ford.

"Honeysuckle?" Elena said with a sniff. "Is that one of your new dogs?"

"Where are they?"

"Who?"

He began to answer her question then paused when he heard whimpering. He walked down the hall and opened the bathroom door, the three dogs bounded out with pleasure. Dylan headed for the stairs.

"Where are you going?" she demanded.

"I'm going to take a shower," he said, then under his breath. "Hopefully you'll be gone by then."

She came into the entryway. "I came to talk to you."

"You can talk to me when I've finished."

"Dylan Flynn I will not have you disrespect me."

He kept walking.

"Come back down here."

He stopped on the landing and stared down at her. "What do you want?"

"I want to know about the child."

"What child?"

"The one you've been hiding."

Dylan wiped sweat from his forehead. "Have you gone senile?"

"Are you going to deny the proof I found?"

"Proof? What proof?"

Elena turned and headed for the kitchen. He softly swore and followed. He found her in front of the island holding up a book. "Can you explain this? A cookbook for children?" She pointed to the refrigerator. "Magnetic alphabets? I even saw drawings in the other room."

Dylan took the cookbook from her. "It's none of your business."

"It's my business if you have a secret child."

"I don't."

She pounded her fist on the counter. "Explain."

He put the cookbook back in place. "I just did. There's no child." He glanced at the clock hoping Jodi would continue to stay away from the house until he could get rid of his grandmother. "Are you finished?"

"When is this ridiculous rebellion of yours going to end? It's time to become a man."

His brows shot up in surprise. "You haven't noticed?"

"What?"

He tapped his chest. "I am a man."

She frowned. "You're wasting your talents on old dogs and tutoring idiots."

"They're not idiots."

"It's time you got married and returned to Flynn and claimed the position that's rightfully yours."

"I think Malcolm is doing a great job and when his son and daughter are old enough—"

Elena looked up at the ceiling in dismay. "How could my only son have produced such a weak man?" She shifted her gaze to Dylan. "I had no hope for Josh and Gwen…but you…you have such potential if you would only try."

Dylan adjusted his glasses. "Are you finished?"

Elena snatched his glasses off his face and threw them across the room. "How many times have I told you how much I hate seeing you wearing these? It makes you look weak. Do you even try the strengthening exercises I've sent you? I've never had poor eye-sight and neither did your father. You must have inherited it from your mother. I know you said you're not a good candidate for surgery, but there are other doctors."

"I'm not getting surgery."

"Then wear contacts all the time. There are some you can wear to bed. Appearance matters. Have you ever seen a warrior with glasses?"

Dylan rubbed the bridge of his nose.

"Are you seeing someone? Does she have a child? Is that it?"

"What do you want?"

"I told you—"

"Lies. You came here already knowing the answers. I've never had a private life with you. You know I'm seeing someone. If you haven't heard it from my mother, Gwen would have told you, so stop wasting my time and tell me why you're here."

"You promise me there's no child?"

He folded his arms.

"Why are you doing this to hurt me? Why are you seeing a woman so far beneath you it doesn't even need mentioning? A high school dropout who works for our rival, do you hate me this much?"

Dylan glanced at the clock again. "Stay long enough and you'll get to meet her."

"I don't want to meet her."

"Then what do you want?"

Elena knocked some of the magnets from the fridge, causing them to scatter on the ground. "I want to know what trouble you're causing. I want to know if she's expecting. Are you playing house? How deep are you in with her?"

"There's no child."

"And?"

He shrugged. "And that's all you need to know."

"Why are you with her? What hold does she have on you?"

He shrugged again.

"I could make her life a misery."

He stared at her.

Elena looked him up and down in disgust. "Or wait for when she dumps you after she discovers how pathetic you are." She walked away, moments later he heard the front door slam.

Dylan rested his palms on the counter and closed his eyes. He slowly counted to ten. He would protect Jodi. This battle was between him and his grandmother; he would not let Jodi be a casualty of it. He opened his eyes but didn't move when he heard the front door open and Jodi's footsteps in the hall. She stopped in the kitchen entryway, holding two cloth bags. He turned to her and forced a smile.

"What happened?" Jodi asked, looking at the magnets on the ground.

"Do you see where she tossed them?" Dylan asked, not wanting to clarify who 'she' was.

"What?"

He motioned to his face. "My glasses."

"Oh…um…yes." She went to the corner. "Oh, but they're broken," she said, noticing the cracked temple.

"It's okay, I have another pair."

"What happened?"

He took one of the cloth bags from her hand. "What did you buy?"

"You don't want to talk about it?"

He shook his head. "Nope. What did you buy?"

"Something for dinner."

"I'll take a brief shower."

She reached for him; he took a step back. "You don't even want me to touch you?" she said in a surprised hurt tone.

"I have to take a shower," he said. He didn't want to tell her that he felt dirty. He didn't want to be touched by anyone, especially her. "I'll be right back."

"At least tell me who she was. Why was she here? She looked very upset."

He spun around. "You saw her?"

"Yes, as I was driving up."

He took a step towards her. "Did she speak to you?"

"Yes."

"What did she say?"

"Good luck."

Which meant she was up to something. He silently swore.

"Why would she say that?" Jodi asked.

He released a heavy sigh. "Because she likes to play games with me."

"Was she your grandmother?"

He nodded.

"And she hates me more than your sister does."

"No, she doesn't hate you. She hates me."

***

There was no child. That was a relief. Elena smiled to herself as she navigated her car through traffic. She could have hired a driver, but she still liked to drive. It helped her think.

And the woman he was seeing wasn't expecting. She had to believe him. If there had been a child, or one on the way, her grandson would have enjoyed throwing that in her face. But he was hiding something else. This new woman in his life had a strange influence on him. He'd been more willing and malleable in the past, but this time there was a new resistance. What hold could she have on him? How had she managed to get her hooks in him? She didn't like secrets. She planned to find out what it was.

***

He ate as if nothing had happened. As if his grandmother hadn't come and smashed his glasses and scattered their fun magnets on the ground. Jodi worried about Dylan's cavalier attitude but didn't want to bring up what had happened. She didn't want to make him unhappy. She didn't want to jeopardize what they had. She wanted to stay with him always. When she had to return home it was always with regret.

She only stayed at her house because of her parents. The large house never felt like a home to her, but being here with him did. What they had was real. She finally had what her parents had. Someone who saw her and cared about her. Someone to lean on. Someone to trust. She only wished he felt the same, but she would give him time.

She was ruminating over this at work when she was leaving a birthday surprise on Joyce's desk. She stopped when she heard someone coming and darted into the closet, then she saw something that would threaten what trust she and Dylan had.

Chapter Twenty-six

It had been two months since the disaster at the Spanish restaurant. Dylan had spoken to his sister once on the phone, but had avoided her since, even when he received urgent texts and pleas from Malcolm, but she'd managed to corner him in the pet food section of the grocery store.

He set the large bag of dog food he'd chosen in his cart. "Say it."

"I knew I'd find you here. You're so predictable."

He shook his head. "Not that. What do you want?"

"You have to stop seeing her."

He grabbed a toy. "Seeing who?"

"You're not stupid so stop pretending like you are."

He pushed his cart down the aisle. "I'm not pretending."

"You can pretend to be blind, but I won't be."

"Blind?"

She nodded. "Yes, blind to the fact that she's cheating on you."

He stared at her. "What?"

"She's playing us both for a fool."

"You don't know what you're talking about." He pushed her out of the way and went to checkout.

"She's seeing Malcolm," Gwen continued once they were outside.

Dylan opened his trunk and put his items inside, eager to get out of the brutal summer heat.

"Don't you have anything to say?"

He closed the lid. "No." He returned the cart then sighed when she blocked him from the driver's seat.

"I'm not making this up. I've suspected for months and I have proof. I knew he was seeing someone at By Your Side then one day I followed him and I saw Jodi with my own eyes. I saw her get in his car and kiss him. She's done it a few times. He also has her initials in his phone and one night, I smelled her perfume on his clothes."

Dylan shook his head. "You're wrong." He moved her aside and opened the car door. "You have suspicions not proof."

"How about Malcolm's word?"

He spun around, stunned. "What?"

"Malcolm confessed."

"He wouldn't."

Gwen nodded, smug. "He did. He said he did it for the company."

Dylan stared at her speechless.

Gwen looked at him with pity. "Do you think you're the only one Gran used to get information? She asked him to do it too, he just uses different methods. And as you can see he has more staying power. Through Jodi he was able to get the information we needed." She pulled out her cell phone. "He even showed me some of his reports."

Dylan shook his head, his voice hoarse in defiance. "But Jodi wouldn't. She knows—"

Gwen's eyes slowly filled with tears.

He looked away unable to see them. He hated to see her cry.

"I know I can be a bitch," she said. "I know I can be rude and a little cruel. But not when it comes to you. Don't think I'm saying this to hurt you. We've only ever had each other. Who has ever liked us just for us? Who hasn't wanted something from us? I suspected something about her from the first day. No one is that naïve. I saw the way she and Malcolm were laughing at Annette's party." She blinked back her tears. "She's using you. You think she isn't tallying up your house, your car, your clothes?"

Dylan shook his head again. "No, she—"

Gwen lightly patted his shoulder. "Don't feel bad for being fooled by her sweet smile and lack of education. She's street smart and knows how to step over people. Malcolm says it's over because he doesn't need her anymore and that's why she's with you."

Dylan gripped his hands into fists, feeling a stream of sweat slide down his cheek. "I don't believe you."

"You don't have to, but it doesn't change the truth. You have to watch your back."

***

Dylan absently poured dry dog food into the metal bowls lined on the floor, spilling some. Rosie looked at him annoyed, but Merchant leaped forward and ate it. He didn't notice.

He wasn't going to ask her about Malcolm because that meant he doubted her and he didn't. He knew she was true to him. His sister was wrong.

Then why did she sound so certain? a devious little voice said. Why would Malcolm lie? He hadn't made up getting inside information about the company. And Dylan had looked at what he'd uncovered and knew the information was correct.

He could ask her, but would she lie? Maybe. If she told the truth and said she didn't, would he believe her? He had to. He needed to. His sister was wrong. Jodi didn't need anything from him. Sure, she no longer needed him as her reading tutor but that didn't mean anything, right?

She was smart and ambitious. What if she wanted the face of Flynn's Fleet instead of the man in the background? No, Jodi didn't think that way, his sister was poisoning his thoughts.

He glanced down when his cell phone rang. He saw Jodi's number and hesitated then picked up. "Yes?"

"I need to talk to you."

He swallowed, his throat tight. "You're talking to me now."

"In person," she clarified. "Where are you?"

"I'm at home."

"Okay, I'll be right there."

He disconnected and tapped the phone against his chin. She sounded worried, anxious. What did she need to tell him? Had she spoken to Gwen? Had she talked to Malcolm to get their stories straight? He shook his head. He wouldn't jump to conclusions.

Nearly twenty minutes later he sat in front of her and waited.

"I don't know how to say this," Jodi said, rubbing her hands together. "I did something I shouldn't have and I hope you won't think less of me."

His throat tightened. What kind of man did she think he was? He didn't want to hear it. He didn't want to hear her excuses. He blocked her out until she said something that caught his attention.

"...and when I saw them together, I couldn't believe my eyes."

His head shot up. "Saw who together?"

"Malcolm and Joyce."

"What?"

"My supervisor Joyce is having an affair with Malcolm. I saw them together in her office. I know I shouldn't have hid like that," she said not understanding his expression. "I was so shocked I didn't know what to do. I wasn't trying to spy or eavesdrop."

"What's her full name again?"

"Joyce Dennis."

JD of course. The initials matched.

Dylan fell back in his seat a wave of relief washing over him. He was right to trust her. He knew it.

"I know it's a shock," Jodi said.

He nodded. His sister's pain was his salvation.

"I thought you should know."

He pulled her to her feet and hugged her tight.

"Dylan, are you okay?" she said concerned. "Your heart is racing."

He closed his eyes and held her tighter.

She hugged him back. "I'm sorry."

Thank you. Thank you. I knew it wasn't you. I knew I could trust you.

"I really didn't want to tell you because I know how much you like Malcolm."

Dylan drew away, anger racing through his veins. Yes, Malcolm was someone he used to trust. Why had he lied to Gwen about the identity of his lover? Why would he use Jodi's name knowing how Dylan felt about her?

He squeezed her arm then let her go. "Thank you for telling me."

"What should we do?"

"You don't have to do anything. I'll tell her."

Jodi bit her lip. "If you tell her I saw them, Gwen's going to hate me more."

He flashed a rueful grin. "Trust me, that won't happen."

Chapter Twenty-seven

He'd been expecting Dylan.

Malcolm knew what would happen after his lover dropped her bombshell.

"What did you do?" he'd asked her. He'd buttoned up his shirt midway after he and Joyce had spent time together in their favorite hotel across town, when she told him the news.

"Implicated Jodi," Joyce said, slipping back into her purple shift dress. "I had to do something. She said they were getting suspicious about us."

Malcolm looked at her alarmed. "Who said that?"

"Don't worry, I'm safe now." Joyce turned to him. "Zip me up, will you?"

He zipped up her dress then spun her around. "Who did you talk to?"

She sat on the bed and put on her heels. "An older woman. She knew about us and threatened me if I didn't do what she said."

Malcolm inwardly swore. That sounded like Elena. He'd told her that he was using a woman at By Your Side to get information, but why would she threaten her? "You should have told me first. It's risky and—"

"She told me what I needed to do. Relax, there's no way Jodi can point the finger at me. I did a lot of her correspondence."

"But she's dating Dylan," Malcolm said, his mind spinning with the repercussions. "He's not one to let something like this go."

Joyce stood and helped him finish buttoning up his shirt. "She told me that you'd know how to handle him."

He stepped away from her, shoving his shirt in his trousers. Damn the woman, what game was she playing?

"Why are you upset? You now have the information you need to leave your wife."

He'd never leave Gwen and his kids. Joyce had just been a useful diversion, but she didn't need to know that. "I told you it's complicated right now. I need you to be patience."

"I've been more than patient," she shot back.

"Don't push me."

"Do you know all that I've done for you?" she said, her heart in her eyes. "All that I've risked?"

"Yes."

"I'm tired of waiting. You'd better leave your wife or else."

"Or else what?" Malcolm said with a smirk. "You'll admit that you're the leak and not Jodi? I'd like to see you be that stupid." He cupped her chin. "Don't threaten me."

But he knew he wasn't on solid ground. He'd done some damage control by admitting to his wife that he'd been seeing Jodi, but now he faced his greatest opponent.

Malcolm didn't bat an eye when he found Dylan sitting in his office. His receptionist had warned him and after hearing from Joyce, talking to Elena and lying to Gwen he knew how the dominoes would fall and Dylan didn't disappoint.

"Here for lunch?" he casually asked.

"I'm here to call in my favor."

Malcolm hesitated, feeling a tinge of guilt. He hadn't expected that. "What do you want?"

Dylan sighed and stood. "Tell me why you lied."

Malcolm walked behind his desk and sat, ready to take control of the situation. "About what?"

"About you and Jodi."

"How do you know I'm lying?"

Dylan leaned towards him, his eyes flat and hard. "Because I know you."

Malcolm swallowed. "Do you have proof?"

"She saw you with Joyce."

"And you believe her?" Malcolm said with a sad smile, although he was shocked. He knew going to Joyce's office had been too much of a risk, but she'd insisted everyone was gone. "The truth is she'll say anything to get you to be on her side. She got caught by Joyce. She saw *her* giving me key information."

"That's impossible."

"No, it's—"

Dylan grabbed the front of his shirt. "Why. Did. You. Lie?"

"This is the only family I have," Malcolm said a little desperate as he felt the strength of Dylan's grip. He remembered becoming an orphan at nineteen and having no other family to turn to. He never wanted to return to that sense of rootlessness again.

He'd achieved his success through hard work and cunning. Berton Flynn had taken him under his wing, seeing the grandson he wanted, and helped arrange his pairing with Gwen. "I don't have the luxury to fall out of line like you do. I have too much to lose."

Dylan released him. "You're following Gran's orders?"

Malcolm smoothed down his shirt and leaned back pleased Dylan had made the connection. "Consider the favor repaid."

Dylan shook his head. "It's not enough."

"It's the only warning I can give. Just wait and see," Malcolm said unable to stop a sly grin. "My relationship with Jodi is going to reveal a wealth of information."

***

He refused to believe any of it. Several hours after talking to Malcolm, Dylan met with Larry in Larry's office and looked over what computer forensics had uncovered.

"I didn't want to believe it either," Larry said. "But there's correspondence for months from her account and on her phone between her and Malcolm."

Dylan tapped his knee. "This doesn't make any sense."

"But how else would he have gotten all this?"

"What did you do?" Dylan asked.

"Fired her of course. It wasn't easy. She denies everything. I've scrubbed and searched files to see if there could be a mistake. But there isn't one."

Dylan nodded understanding the numerous calls and texts he'd received from her, but he hadn't replied yet. He wanted to focus and gather as much information as he could first. Dylan looked through the hundreds of emails then stopped when he noticed the dates. "Wait, this was ten months ago."

"Yes."

"She couldn't have done it."

"Why not?"

"Because she…" He stopped before he revealed her secret. That wasn't his place. "I'll get back to you. Who else knows about this?"

"I fired her quietly, so just the guy who helped me with this."

"Good, keep it that way."

***

She still couldn't believe the accusation. And Joyce had stood by and lied saying that she'd sometimes helped her with the reports, not knowing where Jodi was sending them. It was only when she got suspicious that she told Larry. And it *did* look bad because she let Joyce use her account on many occasions. She had no way to prove her innocence.

Dylan wouldn't respond to her texts or messages. Did he believe them? Did he think she'd betrayed both him and his company?

Jodi worried about this as she cleaned up her parent's dishes. She stopped when she got a text. It told her to meet him outside.

"I didn't do it," she said, walking up to him as he leaned against his car, dark sunglasses shielding his eyes.

"I know. You have to tell them the truth."

"I have. They don't believe me."

He shook his head. "I mean the fact that you couldn't have written most of those emails because you couldn't read."

She froze. "No." She pointed at him in warning. "And you can't tell anyone either."

"Jodi this is serious. This is no time—"

"No. I've come too far for anyone to find out now."

"Jodi."

"No," she said again, adamant. "No one can find out I was illiterate."

"How else can we prove you're innocent?"

She searched her mind. "You're the owner of the company, right? If you don't charge me—"

"It's not that simple. How would that look? Besides, I'm not ready to reveal that I'm the owner yet."

"But you want me to reveal that—"

He took off his shades and tucked them in his shirt pocket. "You have nothing to be ashamed of."

"I did nothing wrong. If I could read, what would you do? Would you believe them?"

An expression crossed his face.

"You would," Jodi said in shocked horror. "You would doubt me, but fortunately, I was too ignorant to pull this off."

"That's not what I'm thinking."

Jodi met his gaze, defiant. "Then fight for me and believe in me no matter what."

Chapter Twenty-eight

Shelley Durant Gillis hadn't been in the same house as her parents for nearly fifteen years. She awkwardly greeted her mother and father, sharing a too sweet tea and stilted conversation with them before she excused herself and asked to speak to Jodi alone.

"I'm so glad to see you," Jodi said, giving her sister another big hug before settling on the living room couch. "As you can see Mom and Dad will be happy for days."

Shelley gripped the handbag she'd placed on her lap as she sat opposite her sister. "I didn't come for them. I came for you."

"Why?"

"Dylan called me."

Fear gripped Jodi's heart, but she managed to keep her voice light. "What did he say?"

"He told me about what you're being accused of by that company, By Your Side."

"What else did he say?"

"That he's worried about you and that you have information that could exonerate you."

Jodi waved what she said away, relieved her secret was safe. "He's wrong."

"Why won't you just tell them that you couldn't have done it, that you couldn't read back then?"

Jodi felt a sudden chill, unsure she'd heard her sister correctly. "What? What did you say?"

Shelley looked chagrined. "Dylan told me..." She let her words fade away, and glanced at a photo on the wall.

"He told you what?" Jodi pressed, desperate to make sure she'd misheard her. She couldn't have said what she said. Her secret had to be safe.

Shelley rested her handbag on the ground and clasped her hands together as if gaining courage. "Dylan told me the reason you couldn't be guilty. He said it is the only way to prove you're innocent." She stared at Jodi in amazement. "I can't believe I didn't know all this time. How did you manage? Why didn't you tell me? Does Mom and Dad know?"

"No," she said in tight voice. "And you shouldn't know either."

"Don't get angry," Shelley said, taking a seat beside her. "I came here to help you."

"Help me?" Jodi's voice cracked in surprise. "Why now?" She surged to her feet eager to place distance between them. "You think I didn't need your help during all those family holidays when I asked you to come over? At those family birthdays where I made excuses for you? I don't need your help now. Help when you feel like giving it to me on your terms. Always on *your* terms. I'm done with that. You can go."

Shelley looked up at her with sadness. "Jodi, if you'll only listen."

"Listen to what? Your rationale? Your side? You're the smart one, right? I should listen to you. I'm being silly, stupid even. Maybe, I am. But I've gotten along this far and you're too late to pretend that you care."

"I do care."

"Why? Because it will be an embarrassment? Are you afraid your children will have an aunt like me? That would ruin your reputation, wouldn't it?"

Shelley stood, a helpless expression on her face. "That's not true. I'm worried about you."

"I don't need your worry. You stayed away before, you can do it again and this time I won't miss you."

"Jodi, please. You're taking this all wrong. I know I haven't been the best sister. I stayed away because it hurt too much to see them, especially Mom. It hurt to see how she treats you."

"And it hurts too much to see you now," Jodi said, then left the room.

Chapter Twenty-nine

A tactical error.

Dylan realized he'd made one the moment he opened his front door and found Jodi glaring at him with tears of rage. "You had no right to tell her," she said.

"Jodi, let me explain. I—"

She pounded her chest with her fist, her voice shaking. "It was *my* secret not yours. All these years I've kept it buried, hidden deep in my heart, afraid that she, of all people, would find out and I succeeded. She never knew and she never would have known if not for you."

"Jodi, she—"

"But that wasn't enough you had to humiliate me more. Not only did you have to tell her about her illiterate sister, then you both tried to manipulate me." Jodi raised her brows in mock surprise. "Are you shocked I know that word? I can even spell it. Isn't that amazing?"

He stepped back and opened the door wider. "Let's talk inside."

Jodi didn't move. "You asked her to come over and pretend to want to see my parents. You knew how much it meant to me and you used it."

"I just—"

"You're arrogant. You both think you're so smart."

He shook his head in regret. "That's not why we—"

"Tried to trick me," she finished in a tone of disgust. "I've spent my life building myself up and you threw that back in my face. All I asked was that you believe in me, treat me like anyone else. As if I was someone who could read. I wanted you to treat me as an equal, but that was too hard for you because you never will. You won't let me escape my past."

"Jodi, it's cold," he said, referring to the breeze that signaled the coming autumn. "Come inside."

"I will never step foot in this house again. And I hope this is the last time I ever see you. You know where you can mail my things." She turned.

He grabbed her arm. "Jodi, wait."

She glared up at him, her eyes a biting black. "I'm glad I never told you I loved you."

Dylan let her arm go as something deep inside him shriveled up and died. He didn't know if it was his heart or hope, but it left him with an anguish that made him go cold. He only managed to nod, his mouth too dry for words, then he stepped back and closed the door unable to watch her go.

***

Jodi stared at the closed door her rage making her skin tingle, tears blurring her eyes. He hadn't said a word. He hadn't said he was sorry or that he was wrong. He'd just nodded his head and shut her out of his life, treating the time and trust she'd given him like it was nothing at all.

Didn't he know—or care—how much he'd hurt her? How much his betrayal had devastated her? She'd felt safe with him. She'd never felt safe before.

She pressed her hand against the door, remembering how his home had felt like a sanctuary. She took her hand away and balled it into a fist. Before him, she'd always been on guard; felt like an outsider, but with him, for the first time in her life, she felt like she belonged somewhere. That she belonged with him. And he'd betrayed her.

Fury, shame and pain warred within her. She wanted to pound on the door and force him to ask her forgiveness, to show her that he cared.

Jodi turned from the door and wiped her tears. She was on her own again, but she'd grown used to it and she'd never trust again.

Chapter Thirty

Elena's eagle like gaze swept across the boardroom, she studied the expressions on the faces of her family.

"Loyalty is something your grandfather prized above everything else," she said. "Today one will rise and one will fall." She paused, taking pleasure in the control she had over them. "Josh will now be the new vice president of operations for his excellent work at uncovering a traitor in our midst." She looked at Dylan. "Did you think I'd never find out about your little side hobby?"

"Hobby?"

"Called By Your Side?"

Dylan stared at Josh stunned. Josh looked away.

"I had underestimated your cunning, but your brother hadn't. I realize that your rebelliousness will never change. Don't come back here." She made a dismissive gesture towards the door. Dylan didn't move.

"Mother," Adelaide said, her voice stronger than before. "I don't think that's fair."

Elena tapped the table. "I decide what's fair."

Dylan shrugged. "Still see me as a threat?"

"I think I've adequately squashed it for now. Malcolm has told me about Jodi." She clicked her tongue. "Such a shame."

Dylan gritted his teeth. "He's lying," he said, casting his brother-in-law a look. Malcolm stared back and Gwen looked at him with pity. "Jodi is innocent."

"I don't care if you believe it or not. I have all the information I need to run circles around your little operation thanks to her," Elena said before she sent Malcolm a secret look.

That look made Dylan's blood run cold as he remembered Malcolm's warning and realized that Malcolm was lying on purpose to satisfy his grandmother's plan to hurt Jodi and punish him. "I don't scare easily."

She stood. "Are you finished?"

He glared at her.

"That's what I thought. I am willing to buy you out, of course. I'm not completely without family devotion. The choice is yours."

She left the room and the rest of the family followed-everyone except Josh.

He leaned forward. "I had to do it," he said with feeling.

"I didn't ask."

"She kept squeezing me and telling me I had to do something to prove myself. She always gave you and Malcolm the exciting responsibilities. I was Dad's son too. I deserved a chance."

Dylan stood.

"Gran was certain you were hiding something like a secret child or relationship. She wanted me to find out more. I thought she was crazy. I never expected to find what I did when I came over to visit. When I looked on your computer I thought I might see racy photos or something, but I didn't find anything. Until I saw an old file that had the By Your Side mission statement. After that I found the rest on my own."

Dylan gripped the back of his chair. "Good boy," he said in a mocking tone as if offering a dog praise.

Josh surged to his feet. "I had no choice. I wasn't even going to tell her at first."

"But you did."

"You don't understand," Josh said, his voice a plea. "I had to. It was the first time she looked at me. The first time she treated me like a person instead of like a piece of dirt."

"And why did you have to drag Jodi into this?"

"I had nothing to do with Jodi. That was all Malcolm's idea. He wanted to get information about the company another way since you were undercover for only a month."

Dylan nodded then turned to the door.

"You didn't just betray Gran. You betrayed us all, but as Gran said, you can fix it."

"I could take legal action."

"But you won't." His shoulders fell. "Just sell the company. Then it will be all in the family."

Dylan looked at him for a long moment. His brother was offering him a chance to make it all better. To make this all end. As if he wanted to go back. As if he was actually losing something. He'd grown used to his grandmother's cruelty, Malcolm's lies were a surprise but not completely, but Josh…he'd never suspected.

Perhaps this betrayal was some sort of cosmic justice. He'd revealed Jodi's secret and Josh had revealed his. But the pain of losing Jodi seemed to hurt more every day. *I'm glad I never told you I loved you.*

The woman he'd loved, the woman he'd hoped to marry, hadn't loved him. The family he'd dreamt of having would never be.

"What family?" he said bitterly. He walked to the door. "I don't have one."

Chapter Thirty-one

She didn't want to see anyone. Jodi stayed holed up in her bedroom, ignoring her parents' pleas and Shelley's messages. Even Cara tried to contact her, but she didn't reply. Dylan hadn't tried to reach her, but after he'd closed the door in her face she had slowly let that hope die. He didn't care and she'd never see him again.

To her surprise, she hadn't heard from Larry about pressing criminal charges so she suspected Dylan had told him the truth. If he had no trouble shaming her in front of her sister, he could easily do so in front of her former boss too.

Jodi buried herself under the covers when she heard a knock on her bedroom door. "I said leave me alone."

She heard the door open and lifted her head to glare at whomever had entered. She gasped when she saw Rania. "What are you doing here?"

"Your father let me in. You look terrible." Rania sniffed and made a face. "And when's the last time you took a shower?"

"What do you want?"

"We can't help you if you keep running."

"I'm not running."

"You can't keep hiding either."

Jodi pulled the blanket over her head. "Go away."

"Have you forgotten the oath?"

"Oath?" she said, her voice muffled by the sheet.

"As a member of The Black Stockings Society, I swear I will not reveal club secrets, I will accept nothing but the best and I will no longer settle for less," she said in a solemn voice.

Jodi waved her away. "Yeah, yeah, yeah."

Rania pulled the blanket back. "Do you think I'm joking?"

"I've followed the oath and I'm really not in the mood for this."

Rania sat on the bed. "How long are you going to live a lie?"

"I'm not living a lie anymore."

"Then why are you still in this house? You can move out. Your parents are fine where they are and you can have a caretaker come in."

"I like the house."

"No you don't. You tolerate it because your parents like it. Because they told you how much it means to them, how many happy memories it brings them. Your sister stopped pretending years ago, when will you?"

"I'm not pretending and I'm not Shelley."

"No, she fought to make a life and live with the man she loves."

Jodi pushed the sheets away and sat up. "Fought? What did she fight for? She left and went to college and her life just fell into place as it usually does."

"Why did you walk away from Dylan?"

Jodi stared, hurt by the accusation. "I didn't do anything. He betrayed me. He closed the door in my face! He's the one who hasn't once said he's sorry."

"Did you give him a chance to say he was sorry?"

"He was going to explain, just like Shelley. He was going to rationalize—"

Rania shook her head. "That's not what I asked. Did you give him a chance to say he was sorry?"

"It should have been the first thing he said. He was wrong."

"True, but have you thought about how this may look to him?"

"Why would it look any different?"

"Do you want him to think you had an affair with Malcolm?"

"He knows I didn't."

"He may start to doubt you."

"Why? He knows I didn't write those emails."

"But you could have had them dictated. You're smart. You fooled him before. You've fooled everybody. What if this is all a trick now?"

"Whose side are you on?"

"Maybe it was all a ploy," Rania continued. "Maybe you were using him. You pretended to be with him so that you could find out what he knew."

"You're spinning stories now."

"He trusted you."

"And I trusted him."

"Then why are you taking the blame for something you didn't do?"

"He was supposed to help me. He was supposed to…he shouldn't have done what he did. I will not be branded as the woman who didn't learn to read until her thirties."

"There have been people much older than you."

"It was a different time."

"And there are people right now. Should they be ashamed? You learned to read at—"

Jodi covered her ears. "That's not how I want to see myself. That's not how I want others to see me."

"Why not?"

"Because that woman was once a lonely little girl with a sickly father and selfish mother; the one who dreamed of college but was too stupid to graduate high school; a person who'd spent most of her life in the shadows."

"I'm not saying what he did was right. But have you said anything to him that you now regret?"

"No, I meant every word."

Rania nodded then stood. "Then I don't suppose you need to read his letter."

"Letter?"

"Yes." She pulled an envelope out of her handbag. "Your father brought in the mail and asked me to give it to you." She ripped the envelope in two. "But you don't need it."

Jodi jumped up, horrified. "What are you doing?"

Rania ripped it three more times. "Getting him out of your life."

Jodi tore the pieces from her. "That's not what I want."

"But you don't love him."

She stared down at the pieces in her hand shocked by Rania's actions. How could she have done that? It was the first letter anyone had ever written her, the first letter she'd be able to read and he'd written it. Now it was destroyed. She didn't trust that she knew enough to piece all the words back together. "I didn't say that."

"Didn't you?"

Jodi glanced up at her. "No."

Rania looked at her with a knowing expression.

Jodi sighed remembering her last words to him: *I'm glad I never told you I loved you.* "I was angry. I didn't mean it like that."

"Have you worn your last pair of stockings yet?"

Jodi shook her head, letting the pieces of the letter fall from her hand. "You're the one who promised me the guarantee. I don't see that happening."

Rania pulled out another envelope, handed it to her then turned to the door. "The choice is yours."

Chapter Thirty-two

Jodi stared at the envelope stunned. Rania had tricked her but she wasn't angry, she was relieved. She had another chance. She sank down on her bed, her pulse quickening at the sight of her name and address written in Dylan's bold hand and then saw the words 'Please Read'.

She opened it with trembling fingers.

Jodi,

I'm sorry. I should have said that first. I didn't mean to hurt you. It was the last thing on my mind. I wanted to help you and I thought your sister would understand. You may not believe this but I know that she loves you as much as I do. We weren't trying to trick you, we wanted to help. But I know it's not an excuse. I can't tell you how sorry I am. Please forgive me.

Dylan

PS: Rosie and Merchant miss you and Gus won't talk to me.

Jodi read his letter through her tears, smiling at the last line. Then she read it again, one sentence standing out to her: *I know that she loves you as much as I do.* He loved her. He still loved her even though she'd said she didn't love him in order to hurt him.

She didn't want to lose him. She didn't want her fear and shame to continue to hold her hostage. She remembered how awful she'd felt the first day going to the Resource Center. How Dylan had at first been impatient with her and then changed. She had to change too. She had to be strong. She couldn't run from this. She wasn't alone. She didn't need to keep this secret anymore because she had someone who believed in her.

Someone who wasn't ashamed. When she thought she'd never learn how to read, he believed she could, when she thought she could never follow instructions in a cookbook, he believed she could. He'd always believed in her. It was her turn to believe in herself.

Jodi left her bedroom. She knew what she wanted. She wanted to be with him. She wanted a new life. To do that she had to shed her past.

She roamed around the house then stopped and sat in the living room of the main house and looked around at the bright vivid blues of the furniture that she hadn't chosen. For the first time the house felt oppressive. She remembered Dylan's expression as he looked around. She now saw it from an outsider's eyes. It didn't matter whether she was in the basement or the main house, she was surrounded by the past: Memories from the life of the former owner's and her parents. She knew she had outgrown it and needed to escape if she wanted to be where she belonged.

Chapter Thirty-three

Dylan frowned at the sight of the orange octopus—its bright color the same as the autumn leaves scattered on his lawn. He didn't know how the dog toy ended up on the couch and it was the last thing he wanted to see right now. Losing Roscoe had hurt, but losing Jodi made him feel as if his heart would shatter. He tossed the toy on the ground then turned on the TV and searched for a movie to watch.

Gus came into the room, picked up the toy then struggled to place it in Dylan's lap, but was too short to do so. He eventually gave up and rested the toy next to Dylan's foot.

"Silly dog," he said with reluctant affection. The octopus had become Gus's favorite as well. "I don't want it." He pushed the toy away with his foot and lay down on the couch.

Merchant and Rosie came in. Merchant picked up the toy and placed it beside Dylan.

He looked at the three hopeful expressions. "Is this a conspiracy?" He picked up the octopus toy and waved it. "I don't want it." He threw it into the other room.

The three dogs raced after it. When Rosie returned with it in her mouth, Dylan briefly pressed his face into a seat cushion and groaned. He sighed. "Whoever said you can't teach an old dog new tricks didn't know anything." He held out his hand in defeat and Rosie dropped the toy in his palm. "Okay, I'll keep it," Dylan said, holding it close to his chest. "But if you tell anyone about this you'll all have to find new homes."

Rosie jumped up beside him, Gus used his doggy steps to do the same and Merchant settled down in front of him. Dylan reluctantly smiled briefly feeling less alone and closed his eyes.

He woke up an hour later, not aware he'd fallen asleep, when Merchant barked and the three dogs dashed to the door. Dylan opened his eyes and heard a car coming up the driveway. He shoved on his glasses and glanced out the window then jumped up from the couch when he recognized the car.

***

She was nervous, but determined not to run away. She'd chosen her last pair of thigh high stockings and a bohemian style white dress. She lifted her hand to ring the doorbell, but the door opened before she could. The dogs raced out to greet her. She bent down and stroked them. "I know I've missed you too."

Dylan gave a snap of his fingers and the dogs finished their greeting then went back inside.

Jodi straightened. She motioned to her suitcase and flashed a smile. "I ran away from home and have nowhere else to go."

Dylan didn't smile back but he opened the door wider.

She stepped inside and set the suitcase down in the hallway. "I got your letter. And I read every word."

He closed the door.

"It meant a lot to me."

He folded his arms.

"I've decided to tell them the truth."

He nodded.

"I realized that I don't want to be ashamed of my past anymore."

He rested his hands on his hips and nodded again.

She threw up her hands exasperated. "Don't do that! It makes me think you don't care. Aren't you going to say anything?"

Dylan gazed at her for a long moment before he turned and motioned for her to follow him.

She sighed, then followed him into the kitchen. He pointed to the fridge where he'd used the magnets to say *Dylan loves Jodi.*

"I know," she said, tears gathering in her eyes. She went forward and reversed their names to read *Jodi loves Dylan.* Then turned and hugged him, shocked by how much she'd missed him. "I'm sorry. I didn't mean what I said."

"I understand."

"When your family finds out the truth about me—"

He released her and folded his arms. "I don't care."

She stared at him, surprised by his sudden distance. "That's what I always found amazing about you," she said a little unsure. "Why didn't it ever bother you? You never made me feel stupid."

"Because you're not."

She took a step towards him. "Thank you."

He held out his hand and took a step back. "Are you here to stay?"

"I just told you, I ran away from home."

He shook his head. "That's not the same thing. Are you here to stay for good? If your mother or father calls, will you be running back to them?"

Jodi paused remembering the painful conversation she'd had with them as she packed her things.

"But you can't leave," her father had said. "We have all this space. What will we do with it?"

"We can still rent it. I just need my own place."

"You already have the main house if you want it."

Jodi folded a shirt and placed it in her suitcase. "It's time I make my own life."

"Why are you abandoning us?" her mother said.

"I'm not. I won't be far and you'll still be able to reach me."

Her mother wiped away tears. "You'll move away and not see us like your sister. You see us as a burden."

"No, but it's time to let go."

Jodi remembered those words as she looked at Dylan now, understanding his hesitation. She saw the love in his eyes, but also the uncertainty. She took another step towards him. "Is that a proposal?"

He kept his hand held out, but didn't move. "Only if you say 'yes'."

She pushed his hand away. "I'm not sure that's how a proposal works." She wrapped her arms around his waist.

"Is it 'yes' or 'no'?"

Jodi rested her head against his chest and could feel his heart racing, his body felt tense. She never wanted him to feel this unsure about her again. "Of course I'll marry you, Big Dee."

Dylan lifted her chin and narrowed his eyes in mock anger. "You know I will get you back for that."

She smiled. "What happens when you count to ten?" she asked, reminding him of his warning with Gwen.

"You'd better hope to never find out." He pointed at her. "But that doesn't mean you're safe from payback."

Jodi laughed. "You have the rest of our lives to try."

Epilogue

Dylan didn't sell to Flynn's Fleets and with Jodi's help he was able to make By Your Side expand at a faster pace than his grandmother's company could keep up with.

Joyce quit before she was fired and stalked Malcolm for six months when she learned he had used her and never planned to leave his wife. She disappeared before he could press charges.

Gwen didn't divorce Malcolm, although she made his life miserable for an entire year. Josh stayed on as vice president of Flynn's Fleets for three years until the constant pressure to compete against his brother's business caused a nervous breakdown, forcing him to quit. Dylan eventually forgave him but their relationship was never the same. Dylan's relationship with his grandmother remained strained, but he kept the door open for whenever she was ready.

Jodi reconciled with her sister and Adelaide became the mother figure she'd always dreamed of, though Jodi still stayed close with her parents.

Merchant passed away at the ripe old age of twelve, but Rosie and Gus were still around when Jodi and Dylan welcomed their first child—a girl. Dylan was never without his cell phone ready to take pictures of his wife and daughter like a proud new father.

"That's enough," Jodi scolded him as she picked the baby up from her nap.

Dylan gazed down at the image on his phone with a smile. "I'm making up for lost time."

"I think you already have." She turned to him then stopped when she saw something on the bookshelf. "What are those?" she asked, pointing to a row of children's books that hadn't been there before. In the apple green colored nursery, the white spines stood out on the wooden shelf.

"A gift from Margery. I just put those up. She said she wanted them to be a surprise. I guess she knows our love of reading."

Jodi nodded, unable to respond because it wasn't the books that caught her attention—it was something on the spines.

Her heart began to race as she recognized the significance of the different letters that ran across the spine of each book. Letters she wouldn't have been able to put together before. She remembered Ms. Rehnquist asking her to take a chance to follow something she initially didn't believe in.

She looked at her husband and daughter, her heart filled with love, amazed that such love could be real. She then stared at the letters again and smiled as she slowly spelled out one word: 'Stockings'.

About the Author

Dara Girard is an award-winning, national bestselling author of more than thirty books including *Sweet Temptation, Midnight Promise, Unexpected Pleasure, Just One Look* and *The Amber Stone*. Dara loves to travel and hear from readers.

You can write her at:
contactdara@daragirard.com
or
P.O. Box 10345
Silver Spring, MD 20914

If you'd like to receive a reply, please send a self-addressed stamped envelope. Visit daragirard.com to join her newsletter and be the first to find out about current and upcoming releases.